LOS CERRITOS

GERTRUDE F. ATHERTON

LOS CERRITOS

A ROMANCE OF THE MODERN TIME

BY

GERTRUDE FRANKLIN (Horn) ATHERTON

AUTHOR OF

"HERMIA SUYDAM" AND "WHAT
DREAMS MAY COME."

———

THE GREGG PRESS / RIDGEWOOD, N. J.

PS
1042
C4
1968

AMERICANS IN FICTION

In the domain of literature the play may once have been the chief abstract and chronicle of the times, but during the nineteenth and twentieth centuries the novel has usurped the chief place in holding the mirror up to the homely face of society. On this account, if for no other, the Gregg Press series of reprints of American fiction merits the attention of all students of Americana and of librarians interested in building up adequate collections dealing with the social and literary history of the United States. Most of the three score and ten novels or volumes of short stories included in the series enjoyed considerable fame in their day but have been so long out of print as to be virtually unobtainable in the original editions.

Included in the list are works by writers not presently fashionable in critical circles—but nevertheless well known to literary historians—among them Joel Chandler Harris, Harriet Beecher Stowe, Thomas Bailey Aldrich, and William Gilmore Simms. A substantial element in the list consists of authors who are known especially for their graphic portrayal of a particular American setting, such as Gertrude Atherton (California), Arlo Bates (Boston), Alice Brown (New England), Edward Eggleston (Indiana), Mary Wilkins Freeman (New England), Henry B. Fuller (Chicago), Richard M. Johnston (Georgia), James Lane Allen (Kentucky), Mary N. Murfree (Tennessee), and Thomas Nelson Page (Virginia). There is even a novel by Frederic Remington, one of the most popular painters of the Western cowboy and Indian—and another, and impressive minor classic on the early mining region of Colorado, from the pen of Mary Hallock Foote. The professional student of American literature will rejoice in the opportunity afforded by the collection to extend his reading of fiction belonging to what is called the "local-color movement"—a major current in the development of the national belles-lettres.

Among the titles in the series are also a number of famous historical novels. Silas Weir Mitchell's *Hugh Wynne* is one of the very best fictional treatments of the American Revolution. John Esten Cooke is the foremost Southern writer of his day who dealt with the Civil War. The two books by Thomas Dixon are among the most famous novels on the Reconstruction Era, with sensational disclosures of the original Ku Klux Klan in action. They supplied the grist for the first great movie "spectacular"—*The Birth of a Nation* (1915).

Paul Leicester Ford's *The Honorable Peter Stirling* is justly ranked among the top American novels which portray American politics in action—a subject illuminated by other novelists in the Gregg list—A. H. Lewis, Frances H. Burnett, and Alice Brown, for example. Economic problems are forcefully put before the reader in works by Aldrich, Mrs. Freeman, and John Hay, whose novels illustrate the ominous concern over the early battles between labor and capital. From the sweatshops of Eastern cities in which newly arrived immigrants toiled for pittances, to the Western mining camps where the laborers packed revolvers, the working class of the times enters into various other stories in the Gregg list. The capitalist class, also, comes in for attention, with an account of a struggle for the ownership of a railroad in Samuel Merwin's *The Short-Line War* and with the devastating documentation of the foibles of the newly rich and their wives in the narratives of David Graham Phillips. It was Phillips whose annoying talent for the exposure of abuses led Theodore Roosevelt to put the term "muck-raker" into currency.

While it is apparent that local-color stories, the historical novel, and the economic novel have all been borne in mind in choosing the titles for this important series of reprints, it is evident that careful consideration has also been given to treatments of various minority elements in the American population. The Negro, especially, but also the Indian, the half-breed, Creoles, Cajuns—and even the West Coast Japanese—appear as characters in various of these novels or volumes of short stories and sketches. Joel Chandler Harris's *Free Joe* will open the eyes of readers who know that author solely as the creator of humorous old Uncle Remus. And there is a revelatory volume of dialect tales, written by a Negro author, *The Conjure Woman* by Charles W. Chesnutt.

In literary conventions and the dominating attitudes toward life, the works in the Gregg series range from the adventurous romance illustrated so well by Mayne Reid or the polite urbanity of Owen Wister to the mordant irony of Kate Chopin and the grimmer realism of Joseph Kirkland's own experiences on bloody Civil War battle-fields or the depressing display of New York farm life by Harold Frederic. In short, the series admirably illustrates the general qualities of the fiction produced in the United States during the era covered, just as it generously mirrors the geographical regions, the people, and the problems of the times.

PROFESSOR CLARENCE GOHDES
Duke University
Durham, North Carolina

December, 1967

GERTRUDE ATHERTON

Gertrude Atherton was born in San Francisco in 1857, and died in 1948. Her father was Thomas Lodowick Horn, who came to California in the 1850's, and her mother was also an early settler. Mrs. Atherton was educated at several private schools, the last being Sayre Institute in Lexington, Kentucky. In 1876 she married George Henry Bowen Atherton, and they lived in Fair Oaks, California (now called Atherton). Mrs. Atherton began to write while still a schoolgirl. Soon after her marriage she published a short novel in the San Francisco *Argonaut,* and wrote her first full-length novel, *What Dreams May Come.* She went to New York in the 1880's after the death of her husband. In World War I, she did relief work in France, and received the Legion of Honor. *The Conqueror* (1902) is her most popular novel, though perhaps not her best work, and sold over a half million copies. Mrs. Atherton was inspired by California life, especially the influence of the Spanish "before the gringo came," but she also wrote stories about American life in other localities and periods, such as *Senator North,* an important novel of Washington politics which also deals with the "Negro problem." She has been unjustly criticized as being merely a writer of "light fiction," but in fact her works frequently attack the vital social dilemmas that concerned American society in the nineteenth century, particularly the impact of the aggressive, hard-working Yankee upon more polished, indolent cultures. Her novels show both a direct knowledge of American society and the results of serious and detailed historical research. She is a first-rate storyteller — hence her popular appeal — and her novels and stories move swiftly and smoothly, without digressions or didactic passages.

PRINCIPAL WORKS: *The Doomswoman*, 1892; *A Whirl Asunder*, 1895; *Patience Sparhawk and Her Times*, 1897; *His Fortunate Grace*, 1897; *The Californians*, 1898; *A Daughter of the Vine*, 1899; *Senator North*, 1900; *The Aristocrats*, 1901; *The Conqueror*, 1902; *A Few of Hamilton's Letters*, 1903; *Rulers of Kings*, 1904; *The Bell in the Fog*, 1905; *The Travelling Thirds*, 1905; *Rezanov*, 1906; *Ancestors*, 1907; *The Gorgeous Isle*, 1908; *Tower of Ivory*, 1910; *Julia France and Her Times*, 1912; *Perch of the Devil*, 1914; *California: An Intimate History*, 1914; *Before the Gringo Came*, 1915; *Mrs. Belfame*, 1916; *The Living Present*, 1917; *The White Morning*, 1918; *The Avalanche*, 1919; *Sisters-in-Law*, 1921; *Sleeping Fires*, 1922; *Black Oxen*, 1923; *The Crystal Cup*, 1925; *The Immortal Marriage*, 1927; *The Jealous Gods*, 1928; *Dido, Queen of Hearts*, 1929; *The Sophisticates*, 1931; *The Adventures of a Novelist*, 1932; *Golden Peacock*, 1936; *Can Women Be Gentlemen*, 1938; *The House of Lee*, 1940.

F. C. S.

To

MY MOTHER-IN-LAW

SEÑORA DOMINGA GOÑI DE ATHERTON

A PRELIMINARY WORD.

As I have introduced in this book a dialect new to American literature, perhaps a word of explanation will not be amiss. It may be thought at times that I am inconsistent in its use, but as a matter of fact no American dialect is more inconsistent in itself. Not only do no two people speak it exactly alike, but no man speaks it with consistency to himself. He mixes his participles, garnishes his verbs with wandering "a's," transposes his pronouns, and peppers his sentences with irrelevant words in a wholly arbitrary manner. He is guided by ear and association alone, and the author in revealing him must trust to her own ear, aided by memory and habit. The law of phonetics is absolute in the dialect of the native Californian; there is no other. Were I not almost as familiar with this dialect as with the English language, I should never venture to handle it.

GERTRUDE FRANKLIN ATHERTON.

TABLE OF CONTENTS.

PART I.

THE REDWOOD.

PART II.

THE MAN.

CONTENTS.

PART I.
THE REDWOOD

LOS CERRITOS;

A ROMANCE OF THE MODERN TIME.

I.

CARMELITA.

"HIJA of a thief! Carmelita Banditita! Go finda your father and robba the stage! Go taka the gold and cutta the throat! Where your mother? Who she was? Who marrying her? Caramba! little black bandit, go steal for the books. We no wanting you here."

"I no am bandit," panted the child.

The teacher, in fleeting respite, was down on the river bank eating her luncheon, and the new-comer was at the mercy of her schoolmates. That virtuous and relative indignation which will struggle to flower in the thorniest human heart under the wind-brought pollen of a poisonous

weed, had opened and sent forth its somewhat
over-powering perfume in a half-civilized ranch in
central California. A band of bare-footed, grimy
youngsters, with the black eyes of Mexico and the
sturdy frames of a casual emigrant grandparent,
children whose fathers counted their stolen chick
ens with their beads, gathered, with loud cries and
angry menace, about a little girl who was branded
with the superior iniquity of an outlawed father.
The child stood with set teeth and stiffening fingers, but kept her small bare feet planted upon
one spot, as if determined to return insult with
disdain, until one of the little half-breeds, carried
away by the enthusiasm of the cause, picked up
a stone and threw it at her. Then with a cry of
pent up rage and shame, Carmelita sprang upon
her assailant, and flinging him to the ground,
dealt him a blow that drew forth the howl of a
lassooed coyote. The others, enraged anew at
their comrade's discomfiture, set up a shrill and
simultaneous yell and with one accord cast themselves upon Carmelita. Kicking, hitting, and biting, she managed to struggle through the vociferating crowd just as the teacher reappeared and

ordered them all into the school-house. The
school-mistress, who was a mild and dull young
woman, the graduate of a country town, and glad
to get a situation of any sort, but who inspired
awe upon the Cerritos Rancho from the fact that
she wore shoes, and a gown of unknown and wonderful cut, gave Carmelita as stern a glance as her
meagre features would assume and bade the di-
shevelled little culprit go to her seat. But Carmelita by this time was in a frame of mind to insult
the sun in his course. Without a word in answer
to her teacher's fiat, she turned her back and
stalked haughtily up the road to the house of the
padre, a mile away.

The padre never forgot that first interview with
Carmelita. He was sitting in his bare, comfort-
less study, endeavoring to write a sermon which
should respond to something between the narrow
temples of these savages he had come to labor
among, when he heard a peremptory knock at his
outer door. Going at once to welcome his visitor he discovered a rigid little figure with blazing
eyes and hot cheeks. He had arrived at the Mission only two weeks before, but he recognized the

child as one of many he had seen trooping at
Pedro Espinoza's heels a few days ago and whose
attendance at school he had then suggested.

"What is it?" he asked kindly. "Come to the
fire, and tell me."

Carmelita marched in behind him, and as the
padre resumed his seat he turned to face a small
virago, who clenching both small hands, gave
vent to a torrent of vituperation against which
his remonstrances were like planks before a flood.
She cursed the children and she cursed the teacher.
She cursed the school-house and she cursed the
books. But above all, with hissing, blistering
contumely, she cursed the padre who was the first
cause in this chain of her woes. Upon his bewildered head she called down every damnation to be
found in the store-house of her ten years' experience. She hoped that a pine tree would fall on
him and kill him, that the current in the river
would catch his horse and sweep him to his death.
She prayed that fire would roast him, and mustangs bite his head from his body. She would
have him sink in a bog like Juan Ferrara, with
only his hat to tell the tale. She would have a

Chinaman murder him and an earthquake bury him. She would have him stuck with a thousand pins, were there only as many in the world, and she would have him stewed in the iron pot with the beans. When breath and vocabulary were alike exhausted, she fell in a heap on the floor.

The padre was startled but interested. Her fire and audacity amused him, and instead of administering a reproof to cement her hatred he poured her a glass of water from a pitcher on the table at his elbow. A quarter of an hour ago, Carmelita would have disdained nectar from his hands, but by this time she was limp, and anger had given place to weariness. The padre made her drink the water, then carried her into the next room and laid her on his bed. She fell asleep as soon as she had recovered from the surprise induced by a white pillow case, and the sun was aiming drowsily for the west when she awoke. When the padre heard her slip to the floor he went at once and led her back into his sitting room. Carmelita, somewhat sheepishly took possession of his forefinger and trotted beside him. When he reached his chair by the fire he put her on his knee and remonstrated upon the injustice of holding him to account for the ignorance and ill-nature of a troop of malicious youngsters, and succeeded in making her understand that his suggestion of the school had been prompted by an interest in her welfare alone.

"But I no going any more," sobbed Carmelita, by this time quite overcome, "They calling me 'Hija of a thief,' and say my father is bad man. He no is thief. He only taka the moneys from the rich in the stage, my aunt she say so. He never been in the prison like Carlos Castro's father, and he no stealing the chickens and pigs, only the gold. He no been hang up like Vasquez, and he weara the shoses like you. He no is low, bad man. He is "——

She broke off, unable to find the word which should express her father's superior social status as compared with the common pig and chicken-thief. Doubtless she would have distinguished him with the comprehensive if unfashionable title of gentleman, but that word was as yet un-added to the Cerritos vocabulary. The padre smiled as he listened to the social ethics of the

world from which he had come,—the ethics which
are the outgrowth of that love of the picturesque
which is latent in every imaginative mind, yet
which so often expires in snobbery—spring sponta-
neously from the lips of a little barbarian of ten.
He wisely made no attempt to warp her admiration of her father, that famous Joaquin Murietta,
for whose head the government had been offering
a reward for twenty years. Disillusion would
come with moral development; let her keep the
one ideal of her barren little life, while she might.
But what he could do for this impulsive and passionate, yet sweet and loyal nature, he would; his
banishment to this outpost of civilization should
not be wholly in vain.

"I will be your teacher," he said, pushing the
black clinging hair out of her wet eyes. "Come
to me every day and I will teach you all that
it is good for you to know. You shall learn
to read and write, and by-and-by I will get you
some books. They make life shorter. But you
must not know too much—not too much. Just
enough not to gasp under the smothering, blinding shame of ignorance. But not too much. A

little knowledge is a strong and consoling friend;
too much an enemy, who, mirage like, beckons us
on and on to conquer city after city,—realm after
realm—until we fall panting and dying—among
the ruins that totter on the thin,—iron,—swaying,
—scandent wall—that divides the Finite from the
Infinite——"

He had forgotten Carmelita. His chin dropped
on his chest and he gazed at the struggling wood
and flame in the deep fireplace, with the look of
one whose spirit has flown eagerly from the dull
monotone of its present back to the chaos of its
past. In that barren room, with the dark patches
on the peeling adobe walls distorted into weird,
grotesque figures by the wizard hand of the fire
on the hearth, he was a strikingly dissonant note.
The bent yet spirited head, the slender, muscular
figure, the aquiline profile with its delicate, dilating nostrils, were those of a man whose family
leaves had bestrewed an old-world glade before
some plethoric "Mayflower" had transplanted
the roots to a younger soil. The head, large
above the ears, and the black, deep-set eyes, were
boldly indicative of intellectual power. The lines

about the finely chiselled mouth, and the gray in
his hair were like outline sketches whose artist
has but indicated the suffering he could paint in
if he would. The mouth, too, had once been full;
what had set and hardened it until passion had
petrified to dogged resolve? And those sensitive
nostrils, no muscular constriction could draw in-
ward their quick responding curves; the man's
face was not a mask yet. About him, in spite of
his shabby garb and his purposely disarranged
hair, was an unmistakable air of high-breeding.
What had brought him to this God-forsaken place
to horde with barbarians and watch soul and mind
stagnate? Even the child on his knee, poor,
ignorant little savage that she was, felt vaguely
the influence of a superior personality. She put
out her hand and touched his.

"Who you are?" she asked softly.

His spirit flashed back from those archives of
the past and he smiled into the serious eyes up-
raised to his own. Carmelita had beautiful eyes,
black as an unstarred sky, and the lashes that
fringed them were thick and soft as the sweeping
moss which a night's sharp frost has painted

2

black. The padre pushed her heavy hair, silky as
spun glass, from her small ear, and laid her hand
on one of his. It was rough and brown, but the
shape was as perfect as his own, in spite of the
blunt little nails.

"Who are you?" he asked.

"I am the muchatita de Joaquin Murietta," she
answered proudly.

"I know; but who was your mother? How is
it you live with Espinoza?"

"He is my uncle, because he marry the sister of
my father—you see? One night ten years ago,
Tia Mariana she sitting by the fire all alone in
the hacienda, making the closes for Juan, who no
coming yet. She hear a noise and she jump up,
because she is alone and she have be careful of the
robbas. Then she sitting down again and begin
to cry. It is my father who is there, right by the
fire. He no say one word, but he putting a bundle in her lap and then he go lika he come, with
no one word. My aunt opa the bundle, and she
finda me, a little black thing—I no am so black
now—and kicking and squealing. That night
somebody he robba the stage. I no knowing who

it is "—with an air of conscious pride—"but the
next morning my aunt she find on the table a
bundle of gold, and on the paper my father have
write—'For the Carmelita.' Three years ago—
four years — I no remember exactamente, my
father coming one night and picka me out of the
bed and kissing me one dossen times, I think.
But he no saying one word excep 'Monica! Monica!' and he cry and cry. After that he go and
I no seeing him no more. Oh! I wish I seeing
him, just one momente!"

The padre put his arm about her and smiled as
he felt a solitary flame of human affection pushing its way among the ice-points in his heart.
"And your mother, chiquita? Who was she? It
was from her you got those hands and ears and
the fine threads of your hair."

Carmelita's full red mouth trembled, and she
shook her head. "I no know," she said. "My
father no telling my aunt nothing. Those muchachos "—her eyes blazed again like young volcanos
—"those muchachos they saying no one know who
is my mother. They say my father no marrying.

But it no is so! It no is so! Oh! I wish my aunt
she knowing."

"I will tell you a story I once heard about
Joaquin Murietta," said the padre. "Put your
head down on my shoulder and look at the fire.
Some people can see stories and pictures in the
coals. I fancy you can, and this is a story with
several pictures the flames would like to paint."

Carmelita, with all a child's delight at hearing
a story, adjusted herself comfortably in the padre's
embrace and fixed her eyes in dancing anticipation on the blazing logs.

"Once, eleven or twelve years ago (yes, just
about twelve years ago), there lived in an ancient
adobe house in Santa Barbara an old man whose
grandfather, many years before, had been a Com-
mandante of the post—in those days, chiquita,
when the Jesuit padres were building this Mission and many like it. For some reason which no
one ever knew, the Señor don Rodriguez Alvarado
chose to live like a hermit, refusing to have aught
to do with his neighbors, and never seen abroad.
With him lived a beautiful daughter, so beautiful
that the young men of the town, in the hope of

having a glimpse of her, used to walk by day and by night up and down the road before the high wall which hid all but the chimneys and the hot red tiles of her lonely home. Sometimes they did see her walking among the weeds and tangled brush of the garden, or bending over her books at the window; but to gain that much they had to climb the wall like thieves, and not a word or smile did they ever win from her. They would toast her in the town, and then, with the wine steaming in their veins, they would run down the road and throw flowers and ribbons and gold chains over the wall; but the next morning they would return to find their gifts trampled in the dust of the road.

"One day a whisper went through the town that Joaquin Murietta was in the mountains. A stage had been robbed and the driver swore that he had recognized the famous bandit; there was something about his erect, powerful form and in his bearing that no one who had ever seen or heard him described could fail to recognize. Two days later, at early dawn, a strange spectacle was seen in Santa Barbara. A poor old man, his white hair flying, his eyes wandering with the aimless glance of one whose reason has crumbled under a sudden shock, ran through the streets shaking his nerveless hands and crying, 'My daughter! My daughter!' People came out of their houses and three or four recognized the hermit. In an hour the whole town was alarmed and the young men went in a body to the old adobe house, half fear-ing,—half hoping—that at last they would speak with the beautiful Monica. Why do you start, my child? They searched the house unrebuked, but no Monica was there. Then, indeed, conster-nation spread like fever in a tule marsh, and every effort was made to make the old man tell what had happened. But his mind had gone, and from his mumbling they could only gather that the night before, masked and armed men had broken into his house and carried his daughter away.

"Two days later the mystery was explained. The padre of a Mission high up in the mountains came riding down into the town in a state of great excitement and told every group he met that three nights before, six men, armed to the teeth, the chief carrying a woman, had forced open his door

and ordered him to get out his prayer-book and
read the marriage-service. He had expostulated
and demanded the usual delay and forms, but the
flash of a revolver in the dim room had put all
doubts to flight. He only begged leave to put on
his musty old robes, and when he returned he
found that a lantern had been lit. Against the
wall like statues stood the armed men. One held
the lantern aloft that its ray might fall on the
prayer book in the padre's hand. Before them
stood the chief, tall and strong as a forest tree,
his fierce eyes flashing as the wind moaned like a
warning voice in the cypresses without, softening
as they turned to the beautiful woman his arm
upheld. The woman, trembling and excited, gave
her vows willingly enough and clung tenderly to
her strange lover. The names these two gave at
that weird wedding, in that silent mountain forest,
were Joaquin Murietta and Monica Alvarado."

Long before the padre had finished, Carmelita
had raised herself from her nestling position and
was kneeling on his lap, her flushed face quivering, her whole form vibrating. As he uttered the
last word she flung her arms about him and cov-

ered his face with a rain of kisses. "Mi madre!
Mi madre!" she sobbed wildly, "Mama! Mama!"

The priest felt the tears in his eyes. "Yes," he
said, "I believe that was your mother."

"And where she is? Where she is?" cried Carmelita burying her face in his neck and bursting
into a storm of tears, hot and wild as a tropical
rain. "Oh! taking me to her. Padre mio! where
she is? *Where* she is?"

"She is dead, I am afraid," said the priest
gently. "Else you would be with her."

"No! no! she no is dead," cried the child, all
the pent-up yearning of years bursting from the
starved little heart in a wild, bitter wail. "No,
no, padre. I want mama. She no is dead. She
no would leaving me. Oh! mamacita! mamacita! mamacita!"

The grief of childhood is terrible while it lasts,
it is so abandoned and so all-possessing. The
red hot drops cut the spirit's tablets like acid, and
woman is often saddened by the memory of her
young soul's suffering. The padre was at a loss
what to do with the convulsed little thing he held
in his arms, so he wisely did nothing. After a

time the sobs ceased and Carmelita's head fell once more on the padre's shoulder.

"I no crying any more," she said after a half-hour's meditation, which the padre had foreborne to interrupt. "Mama is dead. I only will say a prayer to see papa."

"Poor child," said the padre, "life, young as you are, has taught you philosophy. Yes, some day perhaps you will see your papa. I am to be your best friend, you know, and I will say a prayer every day in the Mission that you may see your father once more."

She raised her arms, and putting them about his neck, laid her lips to his cheek. "I love you," she said, "I so glad you coming here and I do it all what you say."

II.

AN ADOBE MANSION.

IT was evening when Carmelita returned to her home, a long, low, adobe building about a mile from the padre's house and standing on the banks of the river. The house was a type of its kind; a line of rooms built directly on the ground and opening one and all upon a porch that traversed the structure's front from end to end; the sloping roof covered with dark red tiles that looked like long, round chimneys split in half; the whitewash within and without peeling off in great weather-stained patches; the deep, low window-seats its only comfort. From the clumsily-raftered ceiling of the large living-room hung graceful ropes of blood-red peppers, pearl-hued onions, and hard, glittering, amber-like ears of corn. Through the open windows shone the delicate green of the willows of the river, and the blue-birds and long-beaked scarlet and orange magpies pecked at their trunks. In the wide, open door-way and on the hard clay floor, ragged, unkempt children of all ages and sizes were tumbling; children with great sombre eyes, like still pools of ink, and the clear-cut features of a cameo, but dirty and hilarious as month-old puppies. Over the stove at the end of the room a woman of immense proportions, dark like her children, but whose every claim to beauty had been routed by the conquering rolls of fat, was frying frijoles and baking tortillas. Near her, with his chair tipped back against the wall, a man with a heavy beard and dark, kindly face sat smoking, and laughing at the children.

As Carmelita entered upon this scene of domestic if somewhat grimy bliss, her aunt swept the hot spoon from the frijoles she was stirring and waved it, dripping, in the air.

"Bueno! Señorita Carmelita," she cried, "where you been since you leava the school? Nice girl you are to blacka the eye of Geronimo Diaz, and no pay attention when the teacher she spik. I no giva you any supper to-night."

Mariana had lived in a small town during her youth, and with that instinct of progression which

is latent in every human breast, she always spoke
" English " to her children.

"I no care," said Carmelita proudly. "I am
with the padre all day and he go to teacha me
himself. I no going to the school any more."

At this announcement Mariana dropped her
spoon into the beans and Espinoza brought his
chair down with a thud upon its front feet.

" Whatte you say?" they demanded.

Carmelita rolled the baby back and forth with
her foot. "I go every day to the padre and he
teacha me out of the books. By-and-by I spik
English lika himself and I reada the story-books.
I no spika to those childrens never no more. The
padre he say they are villaines and he go to punish them hard."

By this time Mariana's face had softened, it had
grown almost respectful. The padre is a great
man in these unlettered settlements, and that he
should deign to educate this wayward annex of
the Espinoza household placed her beyond the
pale of criticism at once.

" Bueno, bueno," she said. "The padre he is
right. They treating you orreeblee this morning.

The teacher she coming here and say so. Pedro, why you no whippa those boys?"

Espinoza gave a grunt and resumed his pipe.

"Why maka more troubles?" he asked philosophically. "The padre he do it all whatte is need; he no like si I interfere."

But Carmelita had her supper.

III.

A BROAD DOMAIN.

THE Rancho de los Cerritos was a tract of land covering some fifty thousand acres. A tradition existed that it had once been owned by a Mexican grandee, hence its possession of name and boundary line; but it had long been known as government land and taken up by squatters. The ground was fertile, but after the many mouths were fed and the taxes paid there was little to lay by, and the squatter was always poor. Meat and flour were dear, for the nearest town was thirty miles away, and he could not afford to farm more than a few acres nor to raise cattle for killing. The hog being prolific was not so infrequent a delicacy, and one or two of the colony had a band of sheep. There is little to spur the energies of the settler in these remote districts. Whatever involuntary prompting of ambition may be felt in youth is soon narrowed to the successful raising of a crop or to compassing an occasional dinner of beef. The Cerritos farmers' one idea of society was to meet occasionally at the Aguitas, a half-way house for the stages, and marking the eastern boundary line of the Rancho. Here they would drink and gossip and idle, with no desire for any-thing better in life; and when unknown men came to gamble their ill-gotten gains it meant to them what a circus does to a country town.

The ranch itself was the very flower of a territory that might have dropped straight from celestial hunting-grounds. Those fairy-like hills, golden in autumn, in spring so rich and so lavishly colored that their dew drops surely held impris-oned the rainbow's jeweled hues, in winter palpi-tating with the very joy of life beneath the wild driving rains and the shrieking of ocean-sent storms, framed valley after valley of sweeping plains, and miniature forests and wild tangled woods of chaparral, fragrant with honey-dew and pink with riotous sweet-briar. In winter the river thundered between its high, willow-grown banks, and in summer swept to the clouds and left a hot, white floor sparkling with widely scattered

gold, and red, sharp garnets. Far away towered
the mountains, like the ramparts about a sacred
park, but clothed in an eternal mist that shimmered like pink gauze under the passing sun, or
quivered as if a dim blue veil in the hot morning
hours, and anon wrapped itself, a gown of olive,
about its peaks and slopes, to fade under leaden
skies to a winding sheet, gray and chill.

In a wide valley peopled with flowers and cool
with spreading oaks stood the Mission. The bel-
fry was crumbling like the bones of a time-worn
skeleton, but the bell still hung, a defiant,
haunting spirit, and called the people to prayer.
The rain-beaten, wind-fought walls were covered
with great blotches of red and green and brown,
and the rude carving in the long echoing, owl-
inviting cloisters was changed and blunted by the
same inexorable hand that had laid those brave
old Jesuit artists beneath the earth they had
wrought. Many a young exile with hot heart beneath his cassock had carved into those yielding
pillars the passionate poem of his buried manhood; many a stern-faced, gray-haired priest had
cut the unconscious hope of heavenly compensa-

tion. But restless youth and stolid age are dead alike, and about their sculptured stories the owls hoot, and the bats sweep, like the lost souls the fathers prayed for.

3

IV.

THE PRIEST AND THE GIRL.

CARMELITA went every day to the padre and her bright little mind unfolded very rapidly; too rapidly, the padre thought, and he soon limited her lessons to an hour a day. This child, with the latent instinct of caste, the germs of a high intelligence, inherited from a lonely, studious mother, yet forever the victim of a sordid, squalorous environment, must not be educated into knowledge of herself and taught to hate the lot wherein the strange, unyielding law of circumstance had led her. " I will teach her to read, that she may amuse herself on the winter days when the rains sweep and the ground is soft," said the priest to himself. " I will teach her to count that she may not be cheated out of her little store when she buys the rags she wears, and I will teach her to write that she may not be more ignorant than her cousins who go to the school. But more she must never know, and her books shall be of the simplest, and least imaginative."

The children of the settlement molested her no further. Their awe of the padre was too great, to say nothing of the fact that they respected the skill with which she had used her fists. When she was fifteen she began to show signs of beauty, and when she had passed her seventeenth birthday the question was beyond dispute. Her face was more square than oval, but the eyes were no longer too large for it, and the tints were brown and warm; her full red mouth had taken decided but symmetrical curves, and her profile had the fine, clear line of her Spanish ancestors. She was above the height of most women, but she carried herself with the lithe, untramelled poise of a sapling that is swayed by every breeze. Of her beauty she was as unaware as of the distant but ardent admiration of the young vaqueros and rancheros who caught an occasional glimpse of her. And their opportunities were few, nor were they ever honored by so much as a passing glance. Espinoza's hacienda was at the foot of the ranch, miles away from the other farmers, and when visitors did come they rarely saw Carmelita. She was always with the padre, or in the woods—lying indolently under the trees, or reading the few books —simple tales from the Bible or natural history, or lives of saints—that the priest had given her.

One hot summer's day when the earth was parched and the sun shone like a polished brazen ball through the stagnant air, the padre and Carmelita were sitting in the dark shadows of the Mission's cloister. Between two of the pillars hung a wet blanket and on the table were the remains of a magnificent watermelon. The padre no longer taught Carmelita, but he was her only friend and she demanded a daily hour of his time. The little familiarities of her childhood were hardly a memory now. With all her affection for him, and longing for some object upon which to expend her eager, unsatisfied nature, she never could pass the iron wall of this man's reserve. Whatever his experience of life had been, before he turned his back upon the world, it had made all demonstrations repugnant to him, and dried his youth forever. Carmelita was probably the one human being in whom he felt a personal

interest, and with what affection was left in him he
loved her; but he was ever the priest and she the
pupil; he the man done with life and she the child
who would never know it. But he encouraged
her to confide in him, and every leaf of her developing mind he had turned with his own hand,
every petal of her spirit's flower he had watched
unfold. The last seven years had changed him
little. A few more gray threads were in his hair,
his eyes were sterner and the line of his mouth
was nearly straight. He labored almost fanatically
in his ignorant, indifferent parish; he had vespers
every evening and mass on Sundays, and twice a
month he preached a little sermon. He could not
flatter himself that he had made much progress,
but until civilization reached these stranded ones
it could hardly be otherwise. And at least they
respected him; his word was law.

Carmelita, who had been standing at the edge
of the cloister, eating her last slice of watermelon,
threw the rind among the reeds of the patio, and
seated herself on a box opposite the priest.

"Padre mio," she said, with her usual direct-
ness, "are there trees on the mountain tall as fifty

men like Carlos Castro si each were stand on the other's head?"

"You mean the redwoods. Yes, there are many three hundred feet high."

"I no believe Juan, who got here the other day; but si you say so, I do. The mountain is fifteen miles away and I never have go so far. But to-morrow morning I get up early and go. It is so hard steal that mustang," she added with a plaintive sigh. "Tio Pedro and Juan they use all the time. But I have him to-morrow."

The padre smiled. Carmelita was the soul of honesty, and tractable in most respects, but she would steal the mustang, and many a ringing invective had her uncle and cousin sent after her, when business called them to another part of the ranch and they found their solitary steed had disappeared. But Carmelita was a privileged character and the wrath was usually expended before her return. The padre, however, always felt it his duty to take her to task.

"That will be the third time you have stolen the mustang this month," he said, "and it is only the 8th. I shall lay a heavier penance on you, if

you do not obey better your commandments.
Why not ask your uncle for the mustang to-morrow? I am sure he would let you have it."

"No; no, I no ask. He always say he need. I
have ask, and it do no good, so now I take, and
that save much trouble. Besides, I no like ask
the permission. I like better do the penance."

She rose and walked slowly up and down the
cloister. In spite of her litheness there was much
of the Spanish gravity and dignity in her carriage, and in her eyes sombre clouds seemed to
hang protectingly above the slowly burning fires,
deeply buried.

"Padre mio," she said presently, "I have something I like say to you—to ask you."

"Very well, my child. But remember I have
told you to guard yourself against curiosity. I
have told you that there are reasons why it is
better you should know little."

"I know, but that no take the curiosity away,
and si you no tell I think all the same, so much
better you tell—no? padre mio."

The padre laughed. "Ask your questions, and
if it is well I will answer."

"I want know this," she said in the same even
tones, although a hotter red had come into her
face, "what ouside this rànch?" Is all like this
—thousands acres, hundreds trees, one man here,
and another far? No are no mens in that world
you have on the map who do something but
ride and farm and sleep and eat? No are womens
somewhere who do something but cook and patch
and have the babies? No is there place where
peoples have something else but to work and feel
tire out? Padre mio, all my life I see no more,
but something tell me—and many, many times it
tell me—that far off, but on *this* earth, there is
somethings better. What it is; *I want it.* It is
si I had something in me that no one want. You
no want it; Tia Mariana no want it, but it never
go away, and many times I no am happy at all."

There was a proud dignity in her tones which
took the pathos from her words. Nevertheless
the padre turned his head uneasily from her and
pressed his lips together.

"You will never find it," he said; "put that idea
from you."

She stood before him, compelling him to look

at her. "What it is I want?" she demanded abruptly. "Tell me."

The padre drew a quick breath. For the first time he felt that the girl was slipping by him into a realm where the influence of priest or friend would be of small avail. He had known many women, before he donned the cassock, but they had required no help in discovering their own natures and the needs thereof.

"Give it no thought," he said sternly. "How can I tell what you want? Think not of what you cannot have. It is sin."

"It no is sin to feel what we no can help," replied the girl in the same calm tones; but the priest knew the pride of her nature and her power of self-control. "We no make ourselfs. I no can help this in me. It never sleep by day or night. I no know what it is, but I *know* it no is wrong, or else God is wrong for make me have. And I draw my breath quick—quick—and want to fly! fly! fly! What I want, is high, far above. And heaven is above and hell below, my father. It no is heaven I want, but something on this earth while I am like I am now, but it must be near to there; I stretch my arms always *up*. But I stay below and it is hell."

The padre regarded her with momentary enthusiasm. "Yes; you would always fly upward; but you will never find your wings."

"Why will I no find them," a hoarse note came into her voice, and a flame of angry protest sprang from the depths of her eyes. "No one in the world beyond the mountains find them? You say millions of people there are in those lands on the map. They all go on, on forever, living in adobe huts, lonely, half-make, like myself; no any," she opened her arms wide, "who—who—have—for one moment—something in here?" and she crossed her arms and drew them slowly to her breast, pressing her palms against her shoulders with the passion she had kept from her voice.

The priest stood up, and the man whose fair inheritance had withered and parched looked into the eyes of the woman who was stumbling through the riotous forests of unslaked youth.

"Yes," he said, "sometimes—for a single—— " he paused abruptly. Of what use to talk the platitudes of the world and of philosophy to this

primitive girl? She would laugh in his face. " I
cannot make a map of human nature for you," he
said after a moment. " If the chance ever comes,
you will draw it for yourself; if not, mine would
be so many unknown figures to you. But I will
tell you one thing that has often occurred to me,
Carmelita. Some day you may learn that the
curse of human nature is imagination. When a
long anticipated moment comes, we always find it
pitched a note too low, for the wings of imagination are crushed into its withering sides under the
crowding hordes of petty realities. But it is this
alien and tyrannical force which gives me my
firmest belief in another life. From whence imagination came, God alone can tell; but back to
its jewel-pillared city it must go at last. It battles
against its bars down here, ever straining upward
to higher conditions, and somewhere, some time, it
must find them. Until the body stiffens it cannot
—but then it must wing its way upward and give
to that spirit it now torments all that has been
flashed before his gaze on earth. I have given
you but a hint of my meaning, but some day you

may understand more clearly—although the pos-
sibility is remote enough, heaven knows."

He turned from her and walked slowly up and
down the cloister. Carmelita stood where he had
left her, her eyes fixed on the sunken stones of
the floor. His words had given her no comfort.
With youth beating in every ardent pulse, the
compensation of the hereafter was no requital to
her. She shivered as if the sun had suddenly
fallen to ashes. Sixty years of nothingness, perhaps, between!

The padre stood before her once more. "A verse
comes to me which was written by a blind poet
on the death of a friend, who, possessed of great
genius, died in his early youth. Take it to heart,
Carmelita, for he might have written it for you:

> " 'Oh, men and women, listen and be wise,
>   Refrain from love and friendship, dwell alone,
> Having for friends and loves, the seas, the skies,
>   And the fair land, for these are still your own.
> The sun is yours, the moon and stars are yours,
>   For you the great sea changes and endures,
> And every year the spring returns and lures :
>   I pray you only love what never dies.'

"You are nature's best-beloved child; she will
always take you to her heart. Go to your flowers

and birds and trees. They may not satisfy you, but at least they will bring you no unhappiness. Forget yourself. There is no hope for you here, Carmelita, and beyond this ranch you will never go. Stifle the desire and save yourself misery. Stifle your own nature if you can, or rich, grand, complete as it is, it will be your scourge."

V.

A CHILD OF NATURE.

THE padre had known whereof he spoke when
he had said that Carmelita was Nature's own
child. She would lie on the ground for hours
among the wild flowers, fancying she could see
them grow, and, although she had never heard of
a fairy, transforming them into tiny beings who
murmured to her of the wondrous lands beneath
the earth from whence they came. The ball garments they wore were stored away in chests of
garnet, lidded with gold, during the winter, they
told her; and if she would put on a squirrel's
coat and scamper down the long, ever-descending
galleries of the earth, by-and-by she would come
to a vast room with a dome like the arching sky,
and on a great glittering, flower-tinted throne she
would see a woman whom the world called Nature.
About the woman's cloud-white body flowed a
shimmering gown, green as the grasses on her

hills; her hair glistened with the greenish gold of corn silk, and her eyes were stars steeped in the blue waters of the sky. Above her throne was a choir room cut deep into the blue of the arch, wherein sang eternally the souls of earth's dead birds. About her, when the ground above was parched or wet, thronged the flowers in gowns the sun had never seen; but in spring she sat alone, her body languid and restful, her soul stilled by the music of that joyous choir and the deep chanting of the fiery ocean that beat against her cool, granite walls.

That the living birds had a language of their own, Carmelita never doubted, and she knew it as well as her own. When the voices were shrill, the lord of the nest was scolding, and to the alter- cation which followed she would listen breath- lessly, her hands on her hips, her head thrown back, her eyes darkening and softening in swift sympathy and indignation. In the spring time, when the voices were wooing and soft, she would lie all night on the ground, her face pressed to some many-nested tree, her loneliness for the mo- ment forgot. She waited eagerly for the autumn, when the birds grew reminiscent in idle hours; and lying in the parched grasses she listened to their tales of far-off lands where flowers were as tall as trees, and birds dressed in robes torn from summer roses, where tawny beasts crouched by moon-lit, reeded shores, and men and women made the very stars sing anthems to their beauty.

But above all things speaking and silent, Carmelita loved the trees and longed for those forests of which the books told and the birds sang. The woods on the rancho were small, and although the willows by the river were beautiful in their drooping grace and rhythmic response to the passing wind, there were no mysterious depths in their twining groves, no solemnity nor uncounted numbers. Carmelita was too ignorant to formulate this want, but her nature dumbly demanded responding grandeur. Now she had heard of a magnificent forest on the mountain! Why had she never heard of it before? But she had no companions to bring tales of discovery, and Juan had found it but a few days ago.

She awoke before dawn the next morning, and slipped out with no pang for neglected duties.

In those adobe mansions the occasional chair and
the mutual bed are quickly dusted and smoothed,
the clay floor demands little of the infrequent
broom, and the open doors of summer give the
window panes a long and stifled sleep. Mariana
cooked for the family, and her two eldest daughters kept the house in order. Until three years ago
a mysterious packet of money had arrived at regular intervals for Carmelita. This she had unhesi-
tatingly turned into the common fund, and been
treated as something of a guest in consequence.
Then had come the report that one Harry Love
had carried the head of Joaquin Murietta to the
government, obtaining the long-promised reward.
After that no more money came for Carmelita,
but the habit of her independence was fixed, and
no one in that good-natured Espinoza household
ever thought of altering her position. Perhaps it
would have been better for her had the long hours
been filled with regularly recurring duties. One
care she invariably assumed. There was always
a baby, and until it was a year old it slept with
her in the little porch room she had always in-
sisted upon having to herself. So long as its
4

small tongue could shape no words she might imagine that the child was her own; and although it might lacerate the very ears of night, it gave her a sense of warmth and human nearness, and she never grudged her broken rest. The present baby was now old enough to address its parents with something like discrimination, and as the next had not yet arrived, Carmelita was lonely.

She walked softly across the porch and breaking a bunch of grapes from its vine made a rapid breakfast. Far away lay the mountains, cold and stern as unhewn rock in the sunless light. But Carmelita looked at them with a smile. There at last lay a new world!

Unable to control her impatience longer she flung away the bunch of grapes, half eaten, and ran to the corral. The mustang raised his head in surprise when she entered, but was docile at her touch. He had the lawless spirit of his country and loved better the hand that took him into devious ways than the one which drove him along the stern path of duty. Carmelita had no saddle, but she was above such petty considerations, and springing upon the spirited little animal's back, clasped his flanks with her strong young legs and flew out of the corral and over the fields toward the mountain.

The ride was a long one, and led over many a hill; but with that deep blue curtain ever before her, quivering in the rising sun, the miles ran backward from the mustang's feet. Carmelita half expected to raise that curtain with her hand, and, slipping beneath it, find herself in a waveless sea of blue; but as she neared the mountain the mist faded and vanished like the scent of a flower too long inhaled. She flung not a sigh in its wake, for where the mist had been, giant trees loomed; cold, stern, glorious, majestic, like a vast army awaiting the word of command. Carmelita had been taught to cross herself when she passed the Mission, or an inclosure for the dead, and now with a quick involuntary motion, born of no teaching, she made a rapid sign on her forehead as she stood in the presence of Nature's supremest achievement. Breathless, awestruck, she ascended the mountain trail through a long, dusky, winding avenue of stately redwoods and fragrant pines. The great unbending branches of trees that might

have withstood all convulsions of Nature and
come down from a mammoth age, stretched out
like mighty arms, so high above that the tall
oaks' crests scarce touched them, so thick that
they threw the road beneath into the cold gloom
of a winter's twilight. Above the crowding saplings, which grew between the parent trees, Carmelita could see the towering masses of mountains catching green patches of light from the unseen sun. She rode past sudden chasms with
long shadows on their slopes, and by serpentine
ravines with their ever-dwelling dusk. The day
was hot beyond the forest, but so deep was the
shade beneath the interlacing branches that in
these depths spring waited for winter and summer
never came. It was wonderfully still, not a bird
sang. Once a deer rustled through the thicket,
but that was all. The sound died as quickly as
it had come, and it seemed as if nothing could
ever break that calm again. They are so tall, those
redwoods, so straight, so still, they suggest an absolute dominion over man and beast, awing them
into their own eternal repose. When storms howl
about them their trunks never bend, only their

topmost, slenderest branches creak one upon the
other in rhythmic protest against the element's
discontent. When fire rages through them it
eats out their hearts, but the charred trunks stand
forever, haughtily defiant. Sometimes there is a
wash-out on the mountain side and then the earth
gives way, the great, sturdy, deeply-striking roots
are left without a pebble to cling to, and the
mighty tree moves, groans, sways, and slides down
the mountain. But not far. Soon he overtakes
a brother whose roots are beyond the first force
of the moving earth, and, resting against him, he
thrusts his feet into the soil once more and remains in his oblique position for centuries to come.

Carmelita slid from her mustang and tethered
him to a sapling, then stood for a few moments
with her hands at her temples, her glance roving
about and above. Between the trees the earth
was thick with green and golden moss, yellow
violets, and clusters of lapis-lazuli-like beads—the
seeds of some wild mountain lily—close carpets of
sorrel, springing beneath the riotous brush and the
moveless tree-roof above. On one side of the trail,
sloping down into darkness, was a gorge of many

platforms. Young redwoods flourished rankly in
it, fed by the rotting trunks of fallen pines. Below their bright green leaves, and amidst the fox-
tails' waving tufts, were beds of scarlet lilies swaying on slender stalks. Beyond, the creek murmured
an accompaniment to the vibrating calm.

Carmelita turned, almost mechanically, and
looked behind her. The forest spread down—
down. The Rancho de los Cerritos was as if it
had never been. She sank on one knee and gazed
long at the grave, noble, colossal trees, with their
strange, insistent personality. Were they a race
of mighty, forgotten men, who once had ruled the
world and for great deeds been indured to trees
that they might stand forever? Carmelita, her
hand pressed against the earth, moved slowly
until her face was near the gray bark of one who
might have been the Emperor in this forest of
Kings. She raised her hands and slid them gently up the trunk. For a moment she experienced
a sense of profound peace and content; the wonderful calm and strength of the tree seemed to
promise her everlasting protection and help.
Then, suddenly, a rapturous cry broke from her

and she flung herself headlong on the ground her hand pressing itself convulsively against the tree. "It lives! it lives!" she cried. "It lives and it loves me! I no more am alone. No more! No more! no more!" She sprang to her feet and placing her two palms against the trunk pressed her lips to the bark. "Some day thou wilt speak to me, O my lover!" she murmured in her soft mother tongue. "Some day thy heart will beat and I will hear it. Some day thy great strong arms will bend down and clasp me to thee." She pressed her face close to the tree. "I *know* it lives," she whispered. "Almost, almost I feel that what I wept for I have. Something has come to my heart and my soul. The padre said I should never find it, but he knew not of this forest where trees are more real than the men of the farms below. He knew not of the lover who has waited for me here since the world began." She looked up to the firm straight arms that spread above her. "Some day I shall find my wings," she whispered.

And the redwood moved not, but towered above her in grand, invincible strength and Carmelita was content.

The sun swept slowly to zenith and onward.
It reached the mountain, quivered for a brief
while in a bath of amber, then plunged to its rest.
But still Carmelita sat with her cheek pressed to
her redwood lover, murmuring to him of her
lonely life, of her mother's fate, of her loved and
murdered father, of her longings and desires.
Once, she left him for a moment to catch the sun's
farewell where the creek parted the forest. She
pushed her way through the fragrant under-
growth and stood on the edge of a precipitous
bluff, overhanging the creek. On the low, opposite bank was a tangle of strange grasses, feathery
and slender, brilliant and dim, redwoods young
and delicate, massive and immeasurable, their
gray bark changed to silver in the sun's level rays.
Now the groves were dark and sombrous, now
light and quivering as the sunlight fell in patches
on the fallen trees. The polished, dusky green of
the elderberry trailed its broad shadows over the
waters, and the red lilies reared their flaunting
heads above the swarming ferns. In the tree tops
was a flood of golden ether; then the sun fled to
the ocean and twilight had come.

"It is all mine," cried Carmelita exultingly. Then she turned to her tree with arms outstretched. "Thine and mine," she cried again, "and no man can take them away."

That night she made no confidence to the priest. If she had found a lover whose arms were compelling, her secret could not have been sweeter.

VI.

A DANGEROUS SUITOR.

CARMELITA descended the ladder and running
up the path a few yards surveyed her work. It
was her uncle's birthday and she had decorated
the house in his honor. Secured by invisible
cords on the corners of the projecting roof were
huge yellow squashes, bright green gourds,
bunches of white corn in pale green sheaths and
waving silk. Festooned everywhere, were long
ropes of scarlet peppers. The willows behind the
house trailed over the dull red tiles of the roof,
the storm-painted walls made a rich background
for bunches of ferns and young limbs of oak,
which Carmelita had nailed here and there with
the hand of an unconscious artist. She loved
color with all the sensuous ardor of a nature,
steeped from birth in the riotous hues of the most
gloriously colored country two hemispheres can
show. She put her hands on her hips and turned

her head from side to side, a smile on her mouth. She was satisfied with her work and beckoned to her uncle to come forth from the living room, whence he had been relegated with orders to remain until the picture was complete.

He came out with his pipe in his mouth and looked at his transformed and glowing mansion for a few moments, then turned and patted Carmelita on the head.

"Muy bonita, muy bonita," he said approvingly, although for the life of him he could not see why it had not looked as well before. "Thou art a good child to take so much troubles. Give to me a kiss, chiquita."

Carmelita gave him a hearty kiss on his bearded cheek. Her uncle was not very companionable, but he was a kind and straight-forward soul and she loved him. Suddenly she frowned and dropped her arms. The willows on the bank had parted and a man was coming toward them. Her first impulse was to run into the house, but she changed her mind and awaited his approach with a haughty disdain calculated to crush boor or prince.

Carlos Castro was the one man on the Cerritos

Rancho for whom Carmelita had an active hatred.
An immense, hairy, muscular brute, he was the
greatest villain in three counties. Every year he
was arrested for horse stealing, but so popular
was he that his neighbors invariably swore him
out. His domineering temper and brute force,
added to a certain rude magnetism, born of his
enormous vitality, won from his comrades an
adoration little short of idolatry. Adjoining the
Cerritos Rancho were large tracts of land owned
by wealthy men for the purpose of cattle raising,
and on the largest of these Castro was vaquero in
chief. No one could fling the lasso with such a
wrist of flexile steel; no one sweep the cattle more
quickly into bands. Every animal knew his
harsh, imperious shout and ran from him. Every
under-vaquero obeyed his lightest word as if he
were an arbiter of life and death. In consequence,
and in spite of his propensity for thieving, he
commanded high wages, and he spent his money
with a lavish hand. Another secret of his power
lay in his ability to employ his own vaqueros, and
he only chose the young men who were willing to
blindly follow his lead. Few of his associates

preferred farming their father's small acres to galloping over level miles after wayward cattle, and
Castro's sceptre was rarely questioned.

Ever since Carmelita's childhood this man had
annoyed her with an open and persistent admiration. He began by following her home from her
daily lessons, and when the padre—the only living man whom he respected—had peremptorily
ordered him to desist, he had adopted Juan Espinoza as his boon companion. After that he was at
the house nearly every evening, but it is doubtful if he had ever exchanged two consecutive
sentences with Carmelita. She openly refused to
have anything to do with him, and her frank
abhorrence polished the point of his ardor.

He strode toward her, his small eyes glowing
with a dull fire like deeply seated lava that
awaits the moment of upheaval, his square, bony
face slowly reddening beneath the hair that grew
from eyes to throat, his great jaws working after
his habit when excited. As he reached the girl,
who now stood alone—her uncle having returned
to the house, thankful that his duty was over—
and received no response to his "How you?" his

eyes involuntarily followed her own and rested
upon the fantastic result of her morning's work.

The blood, thick and hot, swelled to his face
and thundered in his ears.

"Whatte is that?" he cried in his hoarse, fierce
voice. "Why you maka that? You going to be
marry? now? to-day?"

Carmelita curled her lip, but made no reply.
She seemed absorbed in observing the irregular
festoons of her peppers.

"Why you no answerum?" demanded the man
in a tone which all the registers of his voice
seemed struggling to possess. "Why you no answerum? Tella me! Tella me! You going to be
marry? *Who* he is?"

Carmelita glanced at him and for the first time
he moved her to a faint pity. Repulsive and
hideous as he was, it was evident that in his savage, furious way he was suffering.

"No," she said briefly, "I no go to marry. I
never marry" (emphatically), "and I wish you no
speak to me again. I hate you." And she walked
into her room at the end of the porch and shut
the door, bolting it loudly.

But after that she wore a knife at her belt.

VII.

THE DEATH OF A TITAN.

A NEW life had opened before Carmelita in that midsummer day on the mountain. She no longer rebelled against her narrow conditions or dreamed of impossible futures. She could not go to her forest every day, because her uncle's right to the mustang had its weight, but once a week she went, and resting her head against her redwood lover talked to him until the lengthening shadows warned her that frijoles were sputtering in the pan. She always sat with her ear pressed close to the tree, and by-and-by she felt whispered replies. There was nothing wooing or tender in these messages; they shaped themselves to words of strength and courage only, but Carmelita asked no more.

Passionate as was the girl's nature, this love satisfied her. In spite of her imperious womanhood, her triumphant fancy, borne in loneliness, nurtured in ignorance, and the ideal within her, carried her disdainfully above the material plane of the people with whom she lived. This imagination heaped scorn upon the boors of her daily life; Castro with his rude, primitive passion, made her shrink unconsciously from what she had never tried to understand, and the padre she did not look upon as a man at all. Consequently the instinct of sex had never vibrated to a responding chord. Her nature, restless as it was, rivalled the mystery of the eternal rédwoods, and it was easy to persuade herself that beneath imagination no life existed worth the having, that the love she had found completed her being. Strangely enough this love, perfect as it was in its way, never stung the instinct of coquetry into life. She never pinned on a flower that she might be fairer in her lover's sight, never gave a thought to the color of her gown, nor to her developing beauty.

One day she was sitting with her head against her tree delivering a long monologue to the army of subjects who loomed respectfully above her. She had named each of them.

"Antonio," she said, addressing in Spanish a

tree whose bark was peeling, "thy robe is getting ragged; it is time thy Guadalupe wrought a new one for thee." She flung a pebble at a tree of lesser girth who stood beside her lord. "Why dost thou not weave a new garment for thy husband, thou lazy one? If thou takest no more care of his clothes than that, mi amante and I will punish thee. Thou shalt have no more children; for soon even they—Pepita, Roberto, Gloria and Luis"—indicating with as weep of her hand, the modest saplings who stood between the parent trees, "will be naked and shivering when the cold fog falls from the white fields above. Then! Señora Guadalupe—Ay! yi! yi! Dios de mi alma! What—what is that?"

She sprang to her feet, shaking from head to foot. A deep human groan, yet too mighty for mortal throat, sounded through the forest. There was one moment's awful silence, then came another groan, deeper, louder, more anguished, more hopeless. It was as if the earth were parting in twain. Then a tremendous crash awoke the echoes. For a moment Carmelita stood, faint and sick, expecting to feel the mountain rock beneath her feet.

5

Soon she realized that the earth was still, and when neither groan nor crash again broke the stillness, she knew that a tree had fallen. She sprang up the trail, following the invisible wave which had brought her the sound. To her keen ears the fainting note still spoke, and even in this great, pathless, echoing forest she knew that she would find the tree. She had a confused idea of covering it with flowers and chanting a burial service, for she felt as if a kindred life had gone out. She almost sobbed aloud as she thought of the mortal agony which had forced that iron heart to give voice to despair and pain.

For a half-hour she pushed her way through clinging lilacs and sharp-leaved elder, and once she climbed a slender, red-barked madroño. But no new-fallen tree met her gaze, and she sat on a log to rest. In the stillness that followed the crackling of parting branches she distinctly heard men's voices. She was on her feet again at once, shaking with anger. This forest was sacred to her, and the voice of man was profanation. She made her way as quickly as the brush would permit, and in a moment came upon a small clearing.

Three men sat about a redwood, just felled
Where the saw had cut through the tree's brave
body the close, red fibre looked like a great splash
of blood. The tree's head had fallen in the creek,
which, disturbed for a moment, now gushed in-
differently on its way. His rigid, mighty arms
seemed to have clutched the earth in his fall.
Stark, conquered, his æons of splendid calm
ended, he lay in his fall grander, more majestic
and supremer, than the broad-chested mountaineers who had dared to drive their steel to
his heart. For a moment Carmelita stood, white
to the lips. Then, with a hoarse cry of rage, she
sprang forward and confronted the men.

"You no are shem!" she gasped, "you no are
shem to kill that tree? Oh! I wish somebody kill
you! You think God make that tree for you to
kill? Oh Dios! I wish He opa the earth and
swallow you up."

The girl with her tangled, leaf-sown hair, her
blazing eyes, and raised, menacing arm, looked
like a Fury whom indignant Nature had tossed
from her caverns to avenge her wrongs. For a
moment the men stood dumfounded at the ap-

parition; then one of them shrugged his shoulders and gave a short laugh.

"Huh! it's that girl of Espinoza's. I seen her once when I went to the Cerritos after my cow that damned Castro had stolen. You mustn't feel so bad," he added kindly to the girl. "We've only cut down a tree."

"Only cut down a tree!" half sobbed, half shrieked Carmelita. "Oh Dios." She turned suddenly to the speaker. "They cut these trees, this forest, all the times?" she demanded breathlessly.

"Oh no! We've only cut down this 'ere one to make a bridge across the creek. There is a good many quicksands along here, you see, and it's dangerous. It 'll be many a day before this forest falls, miss. There be too many others nigh to 'Frisco."

"I hope I be dead before I ever see another tree fall!" exclaimed Carmelita passionately. "I know, I *know* these trees no were put here to be cut down. They are like mens, and like mens no should fall excep when their roots wither and their sap dry." And folding her arms she turned her back upon the puzzled mountaineers and walked away.

The path was steep, and when she reached the top she sat down on the edge of the bluff and sinking exhausted among the ferns cried herself to sleep. An hour later she awakened with a shiver; the ocean beyond the mountains was sending forth its chilly fogs.

Carmelita moved to the edge of the bluff and looked over. Two hundred feet below her, sheer down a rocky precipice, was a garden of green, a peninsula higher by several feet than the creek that swept its base, and covered with a dense, luxuriant growth of shrubs and trees. From its nave rose a redwood. About his feet clung a myriad saplings as if they would hold him fast to earth; but calm and inexorable the great tree canopied them from his height, a hundred feet and more above the ledge on which knelt Carmelita. Around the peninsula's base sang the creek, tumbling over its rocks in tiny cascades, and behind, towered the mountain, a solid wall of redwoods. Over the mountain drifted the fog, but, so thickly thronged the redwoods, their aisles scarce were wide enough to welcome even so shrinking a guest as an ocean mist.

Carmelita forgot pain and anger for the moment;
then she lifted her clenched hand and shook it at
an imagined city's pigmy swarms. "Madre de
Dios," she prayed, "let the houses fall on the men
who build with the redwoods. When the earthquake comes let it open and take down the boards
to look for their roots. And let the men go with
them and clutching at those roots, old as the
world, useless now forever, hang until judgment
day above the ball of fire the padre says is the
heart of the earth. May they roast there like
martyrs at the stake, and may their fingers grow
into the roots of the trees they cut, that they shall
fly through hell holding them always above their
heads." And having uttered her malediction
Carmelita remembered that she was hungry and
started for home.

VIII.

A HERALD OF BAD TIDINGS.

SHE was riding slowly up one of the hills near her uncle's farm when a horseman suddenly appeared on the brow. As Castro's rough head and huge form stood outlined against the fading sky Carmelita gave an exclamation of disgust and half turned her horse's head. Then pride gave its usual peremptory knock and she rode on, her head turned haughtily aside. Castro rode directly up to her, but no ardor was in his face to-day. His coarse black brows pushed each other into a level frown, and his face was purple with anger.

"I have the good newses for you," he shouted. "You so good to me it is good I am the one to tella you. A great——"

"Let me go by," said Carmelita, "I no want hear your news."

But Castro caught her horse by its bridle, unmindful that her hand went to her belt. "You go to hear me," he said. "A great señor buying this rancho and we all have to going."

Carmelita's hand fell from her belt. "Como dice? she faltered. "But no! That no can be. The ranch is the government's before we take it, and the government no sell."

"So we have think. Oh yes! But it no was so; some one he have a Spanish grant—like with the other ranchos—and a rich señor he buy from him. But he no shall have," he yelled, lashing his whip at the air. "He can say he have the grant but he lie. He forging the grant, and si he no did, the man who give to him have done it. The ranchitas are ours! ours! and we keep si we killing the man who take."

Forgetting Carmelita's presence for once, he dropped her bridle and galloped down the hill to his own hacienda, one of the largest and most productive on the ranch. Carmelita, her head whirling, yet refusing to believe, rode rapidly over the hill and across the dry bed of the river to her home. Excitement reigned between those stolid walls. Espinoza had returned from the Aguitas but an hour before with the news. "But we go

to fighting," he cried to Carmelita as he recapitu-
lated the tale. " We putting our moneys together
that we maka this year and fighting si we no have
bread to eat. Hunter " (one of the " white squatters ") " he going to San Francisco and finding the
lawyer; and Clark he say he have more moneys
this year that he make on two hosses he sell to
the stage; and Castro, he give all whatte he have.
Oh! they no can take our ranchitas. They no
can take!" And Espinoza, the mildest and most
good-natured of men, stalked up and down the
room in a state of indignation which was a refinement of Castro's fury.

Little supper was eaten that night, and when it
was over Carmelita walked slowly down the road
to the padre's house. He had given her everything she had asked for; she did not doubt he
would solve the present difficulty. It was a chill
autumn night; a gray mist, like a wind-stirred
veil, covered Nature's every feature, and as Carmelita came suddenly upon the dark walls of the
Mission they loomed out of the fog, gigantic and
distorted. The mist clung to the padre's windows,
and she found him sitting by the fire in his study

—the same bare, cheerless room wherein she had beshrewed and capitulated eight years ago. He had not lighted the lamp, but the logs cast a ruddy glow on the whiter patches of the walls. As Carmelita entered he looked up with a grave smile.

She sat down beside him and took his hand. "Tell me, padre mio, it no is true," she said.

"It is true, Carmelita, that this man, whoever he may be, will try to take your homes. But it remains to be seen if there is any justice in the law. I cannot believe that this Alexander Tremaine has a grant; it is more than doubtful if one ever was given; but even so, the land reverted to the government long ago, and it now belongs by divine right to the men who get their bread out of it. But this man, having gone so far as to claim it, will fight to the death, and he has money to help him to his end. But I believe that we shall win. Not that right always triumphs in this world, by any means, but because the case is so palpably ours. The men have a little more money than usual this year. I left a small property behind me and I shall sell it and use the money in your cause. I will keep a little, for the children

may want bread, but you can have the rest; I
have no use for it."

"Padre mio! Padre mio!" said Carmelita, "you
are good like the saints."

"I shall never be a saint, Carmelita;" said the
priest with a sigh, "but occasionally a chance
comes wherewith to buy absolution for the regret
that still—still—lives, for the old life."

As was his habit, he had suddenly forgotten
Carmelita and was muttering to himself. The girl
put out her hand again and touched his.

"Padre mio," she said softly, curiosity again
awake, now that her fears were half allayed.
"Tell me what *is* life."

The padre gave a low, harsh laugh, his eyes still
fixed on the burning logs.

"Life, my dear, is a gray plain, whereon are mi-
rages—nothing more. The sky is gray with legions
of escaping souls; the ground is gray with the
ashes of their hopes, their ambitions, their desires.
Life is a panting and stumbling pursuit of what
on earth is not. It is a blind and volitionless
obédience to a prompting that bids us grasp and
hold to our hearts life's most dominant desire—

happiness. We spend our first years clutching
the air with eager fingers, our last, gazing at our
hollow palms. We dream our youth away; we
suddenly awaken and say, Behold what matters
whether our dreams harden to substance, or
whether, shapeless and ghostlike, they flit forever
in the realms of the ideal, since the end of all
things is—Death. We kiss the lips that quiver
forever in our spirit's waves like imprisoned
sound, and picture them rolled back from glittering teeth with six feet of earth above. And before
death comes, what have we found? A rotting
flower where we had sought an exquisite perfume;
a torch-lit cavern where hope had whispered of
the sun's broad light. We tramp in a treadmill,
we are the blind servants of mighty Circumstance,
we cannot walk save as he listeth. All lives are
failures, and yet within each are the seeds of perfect bliss. But the stones have been planted thicker
than the seeds, and no man is given a chance for
equal fight." He left his chair and strode rapidly
up and down the room. Carmelita followed with
horrified eyes the vibrating figure over which the
fire cast weird, dancing blades of light. " It is

only a fool who hugs his personal interest in life, after life has taught him wisdom. It is only a madman who prays that his wishes shall be given him, his hopes fulfilled. We are compounded for some object, what, but One can tell. With the ingredients which predominate in each particular compound we work out our destinies as verily as had each most pigmy act been writ in some ponderous Book of Destiny. Every whisper, every smile, every murderer's thrust, or nation's downfall are but links in a chain, forging and unalterably forged." His white face thrown back against the room's thick shadows looked, for the moment, bodiless as a virgin moon; then he raised his hand with a gesture almost of imprecation. "Of what use to pray that the chain may be rent," he cried wildly, "the sequence broken, the world hurled to chaos in the halt of inexorable law? What else do we mean when we *pray*, pray for that which Circumstance, God's chief steward, sees not fit to give us? The Almighty must laugh in our faces when we put up our puny petitions for a grain of happiness out of the bounty of his universe!"

"Padre mio! Padre mio!" gasped Carmelita, as the priest's voice rang against the narrow walls.

Her tone and words recalled him to his senses, and he went to her side and raised her to her feet. "Forgive me, Carmelita," he said, and his voice had become suddenly thin and lifeless. "Sometimes I forget myself. The terrible mystery of life, the helpless, endless waiting for that compensation we are all promised,—they press too heavily at times. Go now, and I will spend the night in prayer and penance. We may not demand of God that he shall revolutionize our earthly conditions, but at least we may cry for purification and patience."

And Carmelita left the priest to a night whose awful mysteries her clear soul never imaged.

IX.

THE CORDOVAS OF LINDAVISTA.

ALL night Carmelita lay awake thinking of the huge cloud which had suddenly swung above the horizon and now hung low over this peaceful hamlet, ready to burst. It was her first actual contact with the sterner ills of life. Occasionally she had shuddered and crossed herself while listening to a tale of murder done by some desperate, passionate Mexican; and a few years before one of the babies had died in her arms. But the tragedies were tales at second hand, and there were so many babies! But this! this! Suppose, in spite of the padre's hopeful words, it should be true. Carmelita turned suddenly on her face and pulled the blanket over her head. She dared not formulate the consequences, but their very flashing phantoms touched her veins with icy fingers. And if they should not have money enough to pay the law! She knew but little of the great legal skeleton which encases restive humanity, but she had heard that its large maw had a greedy expansion for gold. She sat up in bed and put her hands to her head. If her father were but alive! For the moment, yearningly loved as that dreamlike father had been, she thought but of the gold that had gone with his life. If she only had it now to help defeat this demon who would steal their homes. But she was useless as all women, save to cook and sweep; and poorer than the birds without. She rocked to and fro, dragging her hair about her face, biting the strands in her perplexity. And suddenly a thought was born in her brain. Adjoining the Cerritos Rancho was the remnant of a great ranch which had once belonged to a Mexican grandee in those days when Spain ruled and the country's gold was undisturbed. All that was left of Lindavista now was a solitary hill and the old adobe house on its summit. Once that rambling old mansion had been the scene of princely extravagance; beautiful almond-eyed women with mantilla-draped heads and slender fans, swayed like music by curving wrists, had danced the *son* in the great sala, while gay caballeros rode, clanking, into the court without. But to-day the house was bare as that of the humblest squatter. Gone were the laughing women and eager, hot-blooded men, gone the rich stuffs of Spain, the golden plate, the joy of life. A proud old woman and her withered daughters lived alone, thankful for beans on earthen plates.

Why, then, had Carmelita thought of these people? What good could they do her? None, a few weeks ago. But Carmelita remembered that within the month, a strange woman, heavily veiled, richly dressed, had come to the Aguitas by the night stage and been driven directly to Lindavista. A day later a large wagon-load of furniture had followed her. Soon it was known that proud old Señora Cordova had a boarder who would remain for an indefinite time; but what her name was no one could discover, and as she was never seen, her advent was quickly forgotten.

But Carmelita remembered her in this night of her extremity. This woman, she felt sure, was wealthy and must have sewing for poorer hands. Carmelita could sew, that was her one accomplish-

6

ment; many a dress had her deft fingers made for
the little ones. Once embarked on the sea of con-
jecture it did not take her long to reach the shore.
She would go the next day and ask the stranger
to give her work. The lady would not refuse
when she heard her story. And comforted by her
unquestioning faith in human charity, she fell
asleep as dawn awoke the redwoods.

X.

A NEW EXPERIENCE.

THE Cordovas' house stood unsheltered on a bare, brown hill. Every tree and stone had been sold to keep the wretched family above the earth which seemed to have so much more welcome for them below. The large, one-storied adobe house covered three sides of a patio wherein a fountain lay buried beneath the nettles that had choked it to death, and thistles flourished where palms had been. A dingy, occasional patch of paler tint than the rough earth walls was all that was left of the gala-day whitewash, while behind was not a superfluous article of furniture. And yet the stern old dame who lived there never forgot the splendor of her youth, never acknowledged the poverty of the present. Each day, although biting her lips perchance, to keep back a hungry cry, she had her daughters array her in the decaying satins her husband had given her when his

acres rolled to the mountain's feet. Each day she
left her bedroom and sat on a throne-like chair in
her cold, bare sala and forced her daughters to
serve her coarse bread and potato with the same
state as liveried servants had once set dishes of
gold before her. The youngest daughter, Lucia,
sometimes rebelled against this vain simulacrum
of state which had not even gilded her babyhood,
but the three elder women yielded their mother a
haughty, silent, hopeless servitude.

Carmelita had often heard of this singular
family but never seen them. It was therefore
with mingled trepidation and curiosity that she
knocked loudly upon the heavy door of the Cordova mansion. After she had pounded for ten
minutes the door was slowly unbolted and opened
the width of an inch. A tangled head and one
supercilious eye appeared at the aperture. For a
moment there was a steady interchange of glances,
and then the Señorita Lucia hospitably demanded,

"Who are you? What do you want?"

"I am Carmelita Murietta," replied our heroine,
who had it not in her nature to be daunted by
scorn; "the niece de Pedro Espinoza."

The door receded a trifle and two eyes became visible. Espinoza's name inspired confidence.

"And what do you want?" asked Lucia.

"I want see the señora who stay with you."

"But you cannot see her. She sees no one. And why should she want to see you?"

"I must have sewing," said Carmelita bluntly. "O señorita, let me see her. They say we mus leave our haciendas. A wicked man he buy the rancho, and I mus make some of the moneys to pay the lawyers."

Lucia had a kind heart beneath her rough and soiled exterior, and her curiosity was also excited. She now opened the door wide and revealed her entire limp and bedraggled form. "Come in and see madre," she said, "and if she says you can see the señora I will take you to her."

She led the way through barren rooms, dark and musty behind their thick wooden shutters, and turning the angle of the house, threw open the door of a large sala overlooking one side of the court. The coarse cotton curtains were drawn across the deep windows, but Carmelita's eyes quickly accustomed themselves to the shadows, and she saw that a woman sat on a large chair at the end of the desert-like room.

"Make a bow and kiss her hand," said Lucia, nudging her guest, "or else she won't do anything for you. And talk loud, for she is deaf."

Carmelita made a graceful if somewhat unconventional bow when she stood before the august presence and obediently kissed the large-veined, stringy hand extended to her. The woman before her was not less diverting than startling. Not more than five feet, she must have weighed two hundred pounds, and the crimson satin gown which had been made in the days of her slim, young matronhood, was pieced out here and there with turkey-red calico, vainly ambushed by coarse black net. Her grizzled hair was piled high, two flat curls were plastered between ear and cheek-bone, and over all were draped the remnants of a black mantilla. On the minutely wrinkled upper lip and chin of her fat yet shrivelled face was a silken and jetty growth which many a youth might have envied. Her black eyes glittered in yellow caves, and her back was straight from the pressure of flesh in front. Her heavy, pleasure loving mouth was drawn in a taut bow that never quivered, but the cheeks hung over the corners.

" Who is this girl? " she asked in Spanish of her daughter; "and why do you admit strangers? "

"I could not help it; I felt so sorry for her," called Lucia. " She will tell you herself."

Carmelita raised her voice, and its sweet yet piercing tones carried straight to the old woman's brain. When she had finished her story the Señora Cordova bent her head several times in slow succession, contempt on her mouth.

" That is the way of the world," she said. " The rich take from the poor always. Else would they not be rich. I, however, shall help you. You shall have my silver plate and my pearls—the black set, Lucia—and my Spanish point as well, if need there be." This was said with an air so majestic and so gracious that, involuntarily, Carmelita's heart beat high with hope. " But the things are locked in the great chests that stand in the cellar, and I have mislaid the keys. Lucia will look for them, and until they are found it may be as well for you to speak with our guest. She is kind and will give you something to make.

Doubtless she will be glad to hear of you, for my daughters know naught of menial work."

"Madre de Dios," murmured her daughter, "who does she think cooks her dinner and mends her rags? But come, Carmelita, and I will take you to the señora. Kiss her hand again."

Carmelita bent over the withered hand, for whose brown loveliness a doting man would once have bartered all else that made life dear to him, then followed Lucia out of the room.

"You are not to ask her name," said the youngest of the Cordovas, as they walked down the verandah which separated the court from the house, and paused at a door in the wing opposite the sala. "We do not know it ourselves. She wished to remain several months and would pay well. We were only too glad to have her. Madre calls her 'our guest,' but she knows well why there is meat on the table. The señora has nothing to say, but she is no trouble and looks as if she had a kind heart. I am sure she will give you work—mending at least."

She knocked lightly, but there was no answer. "Perhaps she is praying," said Lucia. "She never

goes to the Mission, but she prays a great deal
and has a beautiful prie-dieu, carved all over."

She pushed the door open noiselessly, and as
Carmelita followed her into the room she drew a
quick breath of pleasure. Darkened as the large
apartment was, its luxury was unmistakable. A
thick rug covered the stone floor, and soft, heavy
stuffs hung from brass rods against the walls.
The deep window seats were soft with silken
cushions and shaded with delicate lace. Beneath
them was a broad divan, and in the middle of the
room a carved table was covered with books and
magazines. Great brass andirons upheld the logs
in the cavernous fireplace and the flames whirled
about their heads like lightning around fusing
stars. The tints of the room were subdued, almost
sad, but Carmelita felt for the first time in her
life a delicious sense of coziness and comfort.
Through parting curtains she saw a carved oaken
bed, covered and hung with a material that looked
like the moss which clung to the stout oak's trunk.

But where was the woman whose magic had
transformed an ugly old adobe room into a nest
rich as the wild lily beds of the forest in summer

time? Lucia nudged with her active elbow and laid her finger on her lips. Carmelita followed her jerking eyebrows, then crossed her hands.

In a corner of the room, beneath a heavy ivory crucifix was a prie-dieu, and on its cushion knelt a woman, her head bowed low on her folded arms. Carmelita could distinguish the slender outline of a black-robed figure, a mass of golden hair which swept the floor, and a little hand that hung, white and slender, over the dark edge of the prie-dieu. She felt an ardent desire to see the face of this mysterious woman; she was sure that it would be unlike anything which had ever entered her life's narrow circle.

Whether the woman had finished her prayers or whether she felt the presence of others in the room, she rose in a moment and confronted her visitors. And verily she might have dropped from another planet, so unlike was she to any one who had ever crossed this valley of San Ysidro. The face, white as an ocean's mist, was crossed at the mouth with a line of red, but no blood pulsed in the thin cheeks. She had the green eyes of California—the limpid, translucent green of crysoprase, and the veiling lashes were brown and soft. She might move amidst the graves of thirty-five buried years; unfaded and unlined as was her face it was fixed with the seal of life exhausted. But with those carven features, and that graceful, haughty poise of head she would be beautiful long after her white skin had yellowed and her red mouth bleached.

Her brow, calmed by prayer, was drawn with a slight frown as she saw the intruders.

"What is it?" she asked coldly.

Lucia took her companion's hand and drew her forward. "This is Carmelita Murietta," she said. "Her father was the famous bandit — Joaquin Murietta, you know. She lives with her uncle, Pedro Espinoza, the most honest man in the valley. She has come here to see you, señora. · Carmelita, you will tell the señora what you want, yourself, no? I must go now and cook the dinner for the queen and the guest. It is my turn. Adios." And she went out and left Carmelita to explain her errand.

The lady's face softened as she watched the beautiful appealing eyes of her unceremonious visitor. The girl interested her at once and she was disposed to be generous before her sympathies were demanded. She took Carmelita's hand and led her to the divan.

"Sit down," she said. "I am glad you came to me. Tell me what I can do for you."

"Let me touch your hair!" exclaimed Carmelita.

The lady smiled and bent her head while Carmelita knelt beside her and plunged her hands into the soft masses. "Is it real gold?" she whispered ecstatically.

"Do you like it? It is not half so beautiful as those great black braids of your own."

The girl shook her dusky head disdainfully.

"Everybody have black hair; but this is like the ice-grass in October, like the maiden-hair when the sun have burnt it, like the ripe corn silk, and like the yellow violets in the forest!" She stood up and shook the glittering waves all over the black-gowned figure, then twisted them into a hard, shining rope. The woman almost laughed aloud; the girl was so unconscious of taking any liberty; of the word *caste* she had never heard.

"It is the hair of California," she said indulgently. "The sun married her one night and we are the result. But do you mean to say that you have never seen light hair before?"

"I see white hair," said Carmelita, dropping her rope with a sigh and watching it spring vibrantly to its separate threads. "The childrens of the white squatters they have stuff like wool, but we no see hair like this by the San Ysidro River before—never—never."

She sank down at the woman's feet and looked up into the strange, green eyes, bending over her. They looked as if the fires of earth were frozen in their calm, cold depths.

"I forget that I come to see you for another thing," she said hesitatingly.

"What is it?" asked the lady absently. She was looking at her with the pleasure derived from a keen artistic sense. Carmelita, as usual, had on a red cotton blouse, open at the throat, and a brown cotton skirt that did not reach her bare, little ankles. Her feet, which had never known a shoe, were dusty and rough, but slender and well-shaped. The thick, blue-black braids lying on the floor, grew from her forehead in a waving line, and there

was a delightful harmony about the backward
sweep of her hair and eyebrow and upper lip.

"You must have wanted something very much
to come all this distance to see me," the woman
continued after a moment. "You may be, sure
that I will do anything for you that I can."

"O señora," exclaimed Carmelita, now fully
recalled to a sense of her wrongs. "They go to
put us out of our housses."

"Who? What do you mean?"

"A man who say he buy the Rancho de los
Cerritos. He say it was a Spanish grant. It no
was, señora. We take from the government and
it is ours. That is the law."

"But are you sure, my dear? It may be only a
rumor—a mistake, you know."

"I only know what everybody they say, and
the padre he hear it too. But we go to fight,
señora. Hunter he go to San Francisco and pay
a lawyer. We all give all our moneys, and it is
for that, señora, I come. I must make some
moneys, too, to help. I no know how till I think
of you, and then I think, perhaps you give me
some work. I sewing very well, señora."

"I will give you sewing, certainly. Sometimes I sew, myself, and I brought some fine linen with me to make into underclothes. But I am in no mood for sewing; reading distracts me more; and you shall make the things. No, do not thank me —I am very glad to have some one to do the work. But I want them made like one I have." She went into the next room and returned with a delicate chemise, tucked by hand, its pattern almost lost in a bewildering maze of lace and ribbon. "I like this better than any I have, I think."

Poor Carmelita! Her hopes had suddenly vanished, like a mirage too closely approached. Her rough fingers could never fashion that tender, intricate thing; no needle had ever been made which would not tear it with every puncture!

"I no can do it!" she almost sobbed.

"So I thought," said the lady; "but you can easily learn. Instead of taking the stuff home you can come here every day and I will soon teach you how to cut and sew them. They are the simplest things in the world when you know how. And I shall enjoy teaching you."

"You think I can?" said Carmelita, drying her

eyes. "Perhaps. The padre he say I can do it all what I want."

The woman folded the garment and laid it on the divan beside her. "Have you a good padre here?" she asked.

Carmelita's eyes flashed with enthusiastic fire. Her hostess had touched a responsive chord. "There no is another padre in the world so good," she cried, "I love him and he love me. He teach me all I know."

Was it imagination, or did those cool, green eyes suddenly unlock their prisoned fires? Carmelita winked her own rapidly; she felt as if they were being scorched. Then a curtain dipped in ice-water seemed to wave suddenly between her and this woman. The voice that answered was colder still. "Yes? You love the padre and the padre loves you?"

"Dio mio!" thought the girl. "I do something no right. What it can be?" But she answered out of the straightforwardness of her nature.

"Yes, we love each other very much, señora. Si he was my own father I no could love him more; and he love me because he no have other in the

world to love. And he no is happy, señora.
I know that. He come from the world, the great
cities far off, and something ter*ree*blay happen to
him there. I know! But I wish I know what.
But he treat me always like the child. He love
me, but I am only the little girl he teach and pro-
tec. When I try to go near, it is like a great
adobe wall jump up before him."

The woman's eyes had recalled their fires, and
were soft and dreamy. She bent over Carmelita,
her firm mouth trembling. "But you must have
given him much comfort," she whispered. "I shall
love you for that—I love those who help others;
they are so few; and I feel sure that you can give
me comfort also."

The icy curtain had lifted and vanished in
vapor. Carmelita put up her hand impulsively
and took that of the woman. "I love you," she
said. "Will you let me kiss you sometimes?
The padre never will."

The woman swept her lithe body downward and
taking the girl's warm eager face between her
little, strong hands, kissed her on cheek and brow.

7

XI.

A PAGE FROM THE BOOK OF LIFE.

THE next morning Carmelita went again to Lindavista and took her first lesson in fine sewing. The lesson was the hardest of her life, but she was sustained by the glory of her cause, and she liked her teacher. Hunter started the same day for San Francisco, and the señora told Carmelita that if he returned with the word that a fight was inevitable, she should have the price of her work on a dozen garments at once.

"There is only one thing I exact in return," she said. "You must not describe me or my rooms to any one. I have come here to get away from the world and I do not wish to be annoyed by curiosity and visitors."

"Can I 'no tell the padre?" asked Carmelita coaxingly. "I like tell him."

"No."

"But he no would noy you, señora mia."

"It is my wish, Carmelita. Will you respect it?"

"Si, si," said the girl, ready to promise anything. "I no tell any one." She pricked her finger at this juncture, and for a few moments her mind did not rise above linen cambric. Suddenly she looked up with a flash of anticipation leaping from the depths of her eyes.

"Señora," she said eagerly, "you come from the world, no? Tell me of it. The padre he no will tell me nothing. What is a city? What are like the people who are there? Oh, tell me, señora. I no know nothing at all."

"Happy you are that you do not. I wish my story were as short as yours."

"But tell me, señora. Tell me! Tell me!"

The lady, diverted by the girl's impetuosity, and willing to amuse and astonish her, filled the morning hours with a vivid and detailed account of a great city's many phases. Of its vice and its crimes she barely hinted; there was no need to spoil the picture; but she told of the gay round of fashionable society, of the splendid palaces rich men built, and the lavish entertainments held therein; of the theatre, the opera, the wonders of

the human voice, and of the marvellous sounds
that men had learned to draw from brass and wood.
She described the busy streets with their gay
shops, their varied carriages, their richly dressed
throngs of strong men and handsome women. She
pictured the great markets stacked with delica-
cies whose names carried no meaning through
Carmelita's thrilling ears; the hotels where whole
families lived suspended in air; the libraries, the
art galleries, and the luxurious restaurants. Her
audience made no pretence to go on with her
work. She sat with rigid fingers locked and eyes
expanding. She was bewildered, fascinated, half
disposed to doubt, yet responding with the instinct
of civilization her mother had given her. The
lecturer was made to recapitulate her descriptions
again and again. Suddenly an angry gleam shot
through Carmelita's eyes.

"And the Señor Tremaine," she interrupted;
" what kind of a house he have? "

The señora looked at her in surprise. " What
do you know of him? " she asked.

" He is the man who go to take our haciendas—
who buy the rancho," exclaimed Carmelita fiercely.

"Alexander Tremaine! I know him slightly, but I don't like his wife. So he is the man to whom I am indebted for my little seamstress. It is amusing to watch the links of a chain."

"Tell me what kind of a house he have," said Carmelita, who was a philosopher in her own way, but not given to abstract reasoning.

"One of the finest in San Francisco. In fact I know of nothing that surpasses it. With the grounds it covers nearly a block and he has probably spent two million dollars on it. The picture gallery is one of the finest in America; certainly there is nothing on this coast to compare with it. He is one of the richest men in California—must be worth $15,000,000 at least. His wife has great taste and has been abroad many times. I do not like her, but I must admit that she has furnished one of the most exquisite houses I have seen in America."

"How he make all that money?" demanded Carmelita. "He work on the farms? or he pan the gold out the creek like the Chinamens?"

"Oh, he did not make it at all. His father left it to him."

"And how his father make?"

"Really, my dear — oh — yes — I believe he
bought large varas of land in San Francisco in
early days, and they increased wonderfully in
value. Tremaine also owns a whole country town
somewhere. His rents are enormous."

"And this man,"—gasped Carmelita, her face
blazing with rage—"this man who have cities and
towns and have a house big like an acre, and a
mountain of gold, this man go to take from us
our little farms? Oh! he no can do it! The law
no letting him. He is thief, murderer—for the
children they starve. O señora! It no can be!
How he is so cruelle."

The lady was puzzled how to reply. Her sympathies were with poverty and suffering always;
but a man surely had a right to buy what land he
chose if he found the title clear.

"My dear girl, I hope you will win your suit,"
she said; "but if you lose, Tremaine will not be a
villain if he takes what the law gives him. You
see he will not get this ranch for nothing; he will
pay one or two hundred thousand dollars for it,
at the very least. And if he pays, he surely has a

right to the land. Cannot you move to some place near here—some other ranch?"

"There no is more Government land for forty miles, 'cept the redwood mountains, and we no can farm in them," said Carmelita sullenly. "All —all the ranchos are own by three or four rich mens who raise wheat or cattle to sell, for they no can use. You say we all are make alike, señora. You who are white and beautiful are make like me with my brown skin and my rough feet. Si we all are make alike, God intend we all have alike. We no pay Him, for the land is His. Why then we pay the mens, or the mens pay and take from us? You no pay for your hair and skin, señora. Why you pay for the land that make the food to keep you alive?"

"My dear child," cried the lady with a laugh, "I cannot reason with you. I do not think I should be pleased if all men were alike. Where would be the excitement of life, the power, the pride of birth? Caste fascinates its favorites, my child. I have no desire to do my own washing or live in a hut exactly like my neighbor's. But let us talk of something else. Tell me about your-

self —your history, your life. I want to know
all about you. Lucia said that you were the
daughter of Joaquin Murietta. Tell me the whole
story. I long to hear a real romance."

"I hate the Señor don Alejandro Tremaine!"
said Carmelita through her teeth.

"Come, come, think no more about him. I am
sure you will win the day." And by degrees she
succeeded in diverting Carmelita's mind, and drew
from her all there was to tell. She was deeply
interested and gratified to learn that the girl had
gentle blood in her veins. That accounted for the
indulgence and sympathy she had felt from the
first. Carmelita, after much hesitation, confided her
own romance, with its unique but steadfast hero.
The subtle pleasure of woman's friendship, known
for the first time, thawed her natural reserve; she
succumbed to its potent and historic influence
and told the tale of that mountain betrothal.

The woman listened with an amazement which
had in it the pungent flavor of a new sensation.
"Carmelita!" she exclaimed when the girl had
concluded, "do you mean to tell me that such a
love as that satisfies you?"

"Yes," said Carmelita calmly. "Is he no strong and beautiful and grand? and will he no love me when all mens are rotted in their graves? I stand under his arms when the rain pour down and it no touch me. I get behind him when the cold wind fly through the forest and I no feel it at all. He take care me alway. I tell him all my troubles and he whisper to me and I no mind. I kissing him and I feel sad and lonely no more."

The woman, whose very memory of love still shook her in the night's long hours, made no further attempt to analyze this girl's simple yet unaccountable nature. There was nothing to do but take her as she was, and enjoy the novelty of the experience. When Carmelita rose to go she held her hand for a moment.

"I wish you to call me by my name—Geraldine," she said. "Who knows?—my mother may have known your own; she lived in Santa Barbara at one time."

This was drawing the line of imagination pretty tight, but it pleased Carmelita. She threw both arms around her new friend, and kissed her on either cheek. "Geraldina—Geraldinita," she said.

"I like the name. I like much better call you that than Señora. And next to my tree and the padre, I like you better than any one in the would I have ever know."

XII.

A WEARY YEAR.

HUNTER returned at the end of two weeks with confirmation of every fear. Alexander Tremaine claimed to possess a deed and grant without flaws and would fight the squatters straight over the boundary line of the Cerritos Rancho. Hunter had placed the squatters' case in the hands of as able a lawyer as they could afford to pay. When, therefore, a few days later the notice came to quit they paid no attention; and the lawsuit which lasted throughout the following year became one of the most celebrated in the annals of the State. The San Franciscans who read its details over their morning coffee had that vague, picturesque idea of the belligerent squatters natural to the city-bred man who regards the country as having been made for shooting and fishing purposes alone. For one who has passed the greater part of his life in San Francisco it is particularly hard to grasp the meaning of the word poverty in its most significent sense. There is so little there. One never sees a barefooted newsboy, and rarely hears of death from want of bread. The city is too young for tenement houses and swarming alleys. That actual starvation should menace any band of people so wise as to have pitched their tents on California's rich abundant soil was a deduction which never presented itself to the average mind; the squatters would have to move on and camp elsewhere, that was all.

But that was a bitter year on the Cerritos. Hope leaped or flickered, only to die again and again. The farmers saw their little hoards slowly diminishing, the padre gave all his store, even Geraldine contributed much of her small income; but she could not touch her principal and the demands upon her were many. She had been rich once, she told Carmelita, but trustees had mismanaged and she had little now. The year was not a profitable one and it began to look as if the scale must soon balance between lawyers' fees and bread for the children. At the Aguitas, good-natured faces no longer gathered about the bar or

fire to discuss the affairs of neighboring ranchos.
Occasionally the men met, but their faces were
sullen or sad, according to their natures, and the
black hopelessness of the future turned their infrequent dram to wormwood. The faculty of
representativeness may not burn brightly in the
brain of the goundling, but there are few so men-
tally clipped that they cannot while grappling
with ruin anticipate the hungry wails of their
children and the despair of their wives.

During the months when the incessant rain kept
her from the mountain, Carmelita divided her
time between Geraldine and the padre. She was
too restless to remain alone, and at home they did
not need her. Above her terror of the future
towered the sense of wrong, dwarfing it as might
an oak a shrub. She hated the man who had become the arbiter of this settlement's destiny as she
would have hated some strange, poisonous weed
which had suddenly appeared in the forest to
strife her redwoods to death. She brooded over
the picture Geraldine had painted of his wealth
and magnificence until it stood as vividly within
her mental camera as if her actual vision had

ached before it. For the first time she began to
feel some regard for Castro. Had it been possible,
the ferocious young giant's hatred for the usurper
was deeper and more deadly than hers. As he
strode up and down the Espinozas' living-room
working and crunching his enormous jaws as if
his arch-enemy were between them and fighting
the air with his hairy iron fists Carmelita respected and almost liked him, despite the repug-
nance which made her very flesh shrink when,
encouraged by a sympathetic flash in her eyes, he
approached too near. But those few approving
glances annihilated all memory of disdain, and
side by side with Castro's hatred the fierce love
grew and flourished. Castro being the acknowledged leader of the squatters it was understood
that if the law went against them his judgment
should shape their course. The case was decided
for Tremaine during the winter, but the squatters
were prepared for this and appealed immediately
to the Supreme Court. The result was awaited
with a torturing anxiety which paralyzed their
energies, and Carmelita grew to believe that every
misery of life had drifted to her corner of the

world and dwelt in the heavy clouds which hung
all winter above the Cerritos Ranch. The sullen
boom of the river seemed ever muttering the tid-
ings of woe, and the lamenting wind that flew
past the adobe walls came straight from the heart
of Nature, breaking for her children. Never had
the rain fallen so ceaselessly. The crops were
almost swamped, and the river's boom rose to
thunder, threatening to leap above its banks and
snatch this people's fate from the hands of Alexander Tremaine.

For three months Carmelita had not been to her
forest; she dared not trust the roads with their
treacherous bogs. An innocent puddle might be
as hungry as a quicksand, and more than one cow
wandered forth that winter never to return.
Geraldine thought it best not to lend her novels,
but she diverted her mind through long hours
with the romantic episodes of history and Carmelita promptly renamed all her redwoods after
the heroes of antiquity. Geraldine could talk with
a certain picturesque swiftness when she chose,
and her ardent young admirer often forgot the
future and fled at her bidding into the past.

When spring came the sun marshalled the
clouds into battalions and routed them from the
field, the river sank, and slowly the earth dried.
But the wind was sharp and the squatters shivered around their wet logs. Within their bodies
the fires were feebler yet, for food was becoming
scarce and more scarce and the rags on the backs
of the women and children were scanty and thin.

"Even si we win," thought Carmelita, as she
crouched by the hearth one day, "we no will have
nothing left but a roof to our heads. The childrens go to die now and we no will have one cents
left to buy good food and make them like they
are a year ago. Ah! los pobrecitos, they are so
pretty and so gay before."

She went suddenly out of the door; it was
misery, in her helplessness, to watch them. The
snow on the mountains filled the air with unseen
icicles; but she was unusually robust and as she
ran down the road the blood warmed in her veins.
The sparkling atmosphere seemed vibrant with
life. It touched her nerves with electric thrill.
She threw back her head and inhaled deep
draughts and for the moment reeled as if a golden

pungent liquor had fired her throat.   Nature was
awake and dominant once more.   Already she
was standing before a great mirror below smiling
at her radiant face while handmaidens girded
her loins with the flowered robe and laid the man-
tle of green on her shoulders.   In the radiating
galleries the flowers yawned in their cells and
awoke, then sprang eagerly to the golden chests
and danced into their gala gowns.   The soul-birds
choired memoirs of amorous springs, and Nature
sighed in her fair triumphant isolation.

When Carmelita reached the Mission, she went
within and said a prayer, then sought the padre.
He was not in his house, and she wandered back
to the Mission and strayed through the cells and
cloisters.   In one room was a chest of battered
saints, the nearest approach to dolls she had ever
known.   Many an hour she had spent with them
in her childhood, and she had a fancy to look at
them once more.   She took out the poor old saints
and stood them on end and told them the legends
of their nativity.   But the cloisters had cast their
shadows over her, the farce was a hollow one, and
she soon re-buried the saints decently in their
8

sepulchre and dropped the lid above them. Then she rummaged through another chest. She remembered that she had once found some curious old picture books whose glaring colors had inspired her with a firm and lasting contempt for the simulator of Nature. Among the mass of rubbish a bit of blue paper suddenly caught her eye, and she took it to the window, the better to decipher the faded words, written in Spanish.

"This is to certify that Juan Arguello, son of José Maria and Carlotta Arguello, was this day baptized in the Mission of San Ysidro, in the coasts of California. June the 8th, 1780.

"FRANCIS JUNIPERO SERRA."

Unbooked as Carmelita was in the minor results of civilization, instinct told her that this bit of old paper, signed by a famous name, had its value and her heart throbbed with hope. She might be able to sell it and buy clothes for the children. At all events she would consult the padre.

She thrust it into her blouse and rambling through the church once more passed out on to the wide porch with its sunken floor and tumbling pil-

lars. She stood for a moment shading her eyes
with her hand. Not a house could be seen. The
broad expanse of land, green with the recent coming of spring and sparkling with bright, awakening
eyes, undulated away like an arrested sea to the
distant snow-touched blue-veiled mountains. Carmelita locked her hands above her eyes with a
quick angry sob. It was all so beautiful and
peaceful. How could Nature open her chests and
don her jewels and flaunting robes and smile
and smirk at her reflection in the stars above
when she had denied her children food? For a
moment Carmelita almost hated that capricious
incomprehensible empress of all men's destiny.

She dropped her hands with an impatient movement of her head and took the certificate from
her bosom. Did gold lie behind that bit of paper?
If the padre thought so she would have her uncle
give it to the stage driver to sell in the nearest
town. An inarticulate murmuring caught her ear
and she lifted her head, recognizing the sound.
On the edge of the porch in the shadow of one of
the pillars couched an object which tradition said
was once a man. A shrunken form shaking with

the hideous palsy of senile age; bleached well-
nigh sightless eye-balls wandering vacantly in their
reddened caverns; scattered strands of lank white
hair falling grimily over parchment-like skin,
scorched and furrowed and beaten with the suns
and storms of more than a century. And yet he
had his fame! He had helped lay the corner stone
of the decaying Mission which forged his one con-
necting link with a forgotten past and he had
never been off the Cerritos Rancho! As the evening
wind fluttered the blue paper between Carmelita's
fingers he made a feeble lunge at it, his toothless
gums working voraciously, a faint leer overspread-
ing his ghostly features. All other senses mouldy
with the decay of generations, appetite reigned
alone, and the one impulse left in the pulp of what
had been his brain was to eat whatever fell within
the range of the pale night lamps of his vision.

Carmelita put the paper in her dress again.
" No, no, you no can have," she said to the old In-
dian. " But come to the house of the padre.
Perhaps I find some frijoles in the pot."

The words were given to the wind, for he had
forgotten the sounds of the world before her

tongue had learned its use, but they were accompanied by a gesture he understood, and he dragged himself up by the pillar and tottered after her.

As she turned the corner of the Mission, she came suddenly upon the padre. He had oldened more during the past year than in all the preceding nine, but Carmelita had never seen him look as he looked to-day. She threw out her hands as if warding off a blow, then covering her eyes cowered before him.

"It is all over," he said. "The Supreme Court has decided for Tremaine. The rich man has conquered and you must go."

He passed her and went into the Mission, and Carmelita, obeying a blind instinct, flew down the road to her home. But not to the house. She ran to the corral and bridling the mustang sprang on its back and sped to the mountain. On and on she dashed, over hill and field, forgetful of bogs, regardless of angry cattle, until the mountain rose above her. Up the soft trail she toiled, until, taking pity on the panting protesting mustang, she sprang to the ground and finished the journey on foot, pulling herself upward by the chaparral

and young trees until at last she stood beneath
her Redwood. With a cry that rang through
those winter-hushed aisles she sprang forward
and flung her arms against him, then slipped to
the ground, her embrace unrelaxed.

"Oh, speak to me! speak to me!" she cried
with imperious despair. "I go where I can see
you no more. For we going! we going! Oh, thou
art so strong and so calm lift me up in thine
arms above this awful world. O mi amigo! mi
amigo! the children they no have roofs to their
heads! They go to die in the mud!"

And the wind sighed through the Redwood's
branches and shook down the raindrops like a
shower of tears on Carmelita's head.

INTERLUDE.

SAN FRANCISCO.

INTERLUDE.

SAN FRANCISCO.

LIGHT streamed from the windows of a great house high on one of San Francisco's hills. The fog lay thick in the city's valleys but only touched its crests. Those brave enough to sit on the mist-wreathed dummies glided up the steep hill-sides through white calm seas into a curve of starry dark-blue night. On the lower city rested the luminous ocean pierced by the white swords of the electric lights; a flashing glimpse of a weird night world, and again they plunged into waveless deeps. Again they rose and again went down.

Mrs. Tremaine gave four balls during the season, and one directly after Lent as if to waft that period of fashionable penance down the archives of memory as quickly as possible. No one received so few regrets, and her claim to the leadership of San Francisco's society was seldom disputed. And in truth she merited her success, for no woman in

California was more clever than she, and Nature
had equipped her with a dainty beauty as if intending her to be a miniature queen in a miniature
world. Fortune had been as lavish with her gifts.
Mrs. Tremaine's wealth and position—both cor-
relative with the '50's, and placing her, consequently, among the old families of California—
gave her a subtle and unassailable power which
none knew better how to wield. She was too
bright not to be exclusive in this land of sudden
fortunes and her visiting list was as menacing and
responsible as the Decalogue. Moreover she knew
how to entertain, and received from Paris two
trousseaux a year for other women to copy.

A great English journalist was one of the distinguished guests of the post-lenten entertainment
and Mrs. Tremaine was giving him a generous
share of her mathematical yet charming smiles.
As he watched her standing at the head of her
great ball-room with its thousand globes of light,
and its mirrored walls reflecting the scene into
dazzling infinity he wondered if all California
women were as beautiful and as chilling as she.
The rich warm tints of her russet gold hair made

the skin of her cheek and throat most white and cool. The pouting narrow bow of her mouth defied yet subtly harmonized with the cold gray eyes whose steady steelly gleams again warred with the soft pattering voice and babyish lisp.

"She is as wooing as a bird in spring time, and as tender as a domestic kitten," thought the journalist, "but she is as cold as a March dawn, and money and power are her only passions."

"This ball is really a celebration," she was lisping meanwhile. "We have just won a law-suit which has annoyed us for over a year."

"Yes? I am glad to be here to congratulate you. Is it about a mine?" he asked with the true Anglo-Saxon idea that concrete gold must figure in every transaction of the Californian.

"No, not a mine," she said folding and opening her fan with a little graceful curve of the wrist— the journalist noticed that she kept her thumb outward as Spanish women do—"Mr. Tremaine bought a large tract of land—about fifty thousand acres—in Central California, over thirteen months ago, and there were a lot of squatters on it who refused to leave. You see, the Mexican who had obtained a grant for it in the days of the Spanish dominion had gone back to his own country and forgotten all about it. But his grandson found the grant one day in an old desk, and sent it to a San Francisco lawyer, asking him to sell the land. The lawyer happened to be ours, and knowing that my husband wished to invest some money he mentioned the subject to him. As it chanced Mr. Tremaine had once driven through the ranch on his way to Southern California and been much impressed with its beauty. So he bought it at once, intending to turn it into a sort of English park, stock it with game, and build a big house, wherein we could entertain during the spring and fall. (At least those were my suggestions. Do not you think they were original?) It would be so interesting to take one's friends down in a special train and to entertain them in old Spanish style so far from town. But it seems that a lot of native Californians and half breeds and emigrants had 'squatted'—I suppose you understand our uncouth Americanisms—on the ranch, thinking it was Government land. They refused to go, insisting that the grant was a forgery, and you have no idea of the trouble they have given us. Tremaine has spent a small fortune fighting them, but now both courts have decided in our favor and they must go. It is annoying that they did not go at once, however; we might have the house built by this time."

The journalist looked down at the gold brocade which seemed cruelly stiff for the soft dainty figure, and at the diamonds that covered her neck from throat to the delicate rise of her bust.

"And what will the miserable wretches do?" he asked, for he came from the land where poverty sits supreme on her rag-draped throne.

Mrs. Tremaine opened her softly valenced eyes, "Do? Why they will have to go somewhere else; that is all."

"Did it ever occur to you that these people may be suddenly left without bread to eat or the wherewith to build another roof above their heads?" he asked, not from a desire to rebuke her, but out of curiosity to sound her nature. Moreover he had the slow indulgent English voice, which blunted every sting.

She gave a little pout. "What nonsense! There

are plenty of trees—or mud rather, for that is
what they make their houses of — adobe, you
know. And they always eat beans, and beans are
cheap. I never eat them, but I am sure they are.
Tremaine will probably take· them down a barrel
or two of flour and some woollen shirts. He is
very good-natured."

The journalist was aghast. He saw that she
had not an approximate idea of poverty or suffering. Did he give his imagination wings and draw
with letters of fire the fate of those homeless
outcasts, she would stifle a yawn and vote him a
bore. He regarded her with much curiosity.

"And the warm weather is coming now," she
babbled on, "so they won't mind sleeping out of
doors—for the matter of that there are always
sheds in the country."

"But I thought middle and southern California
were very hot during the summer?"

"Yes; I believe so; but those sort of people—
Mexicans, you know—never mind hot weather.
They muffle themselves up in woollen comforters
in summer on the principle that what will keep
out the cold must also exclude the heat."

Then several late comers claimed her attention, and the journalist strolled through the beautiful rooms in search of his host.

*   *   *   *   *   *

Alexander Tremaine was walking up and down his library, his hands thrust almost savagely in his pockets, his heavy eyes dwelling on many things besides his luxurious surroundings. The music crept like a sigh through the thick portières and the light brilliance of his wife's entertainment seemed to turn ever and recede before it reached the doors of this dark book-lined room. He was a young man, thirty-six at most, but enthusiasm had left his eyes and the expression of his mouth was generally listless or cynical. His heavy lids gave him an appearance of extreme physical and mental languor until a close observer looked beneath and was startled by the latent power in those light cold blue eyes or surprised to meet a humorous twinkle. His black heavy brows, whose occasional long hair defied the brush, added to the sullen repose of his face but seemed to curve to a thread when he smiled. A prominent nose and square chin gave great dignity to his expression, and his tall figure was erect and stalwart. His closely cut black hair had a certain vitality in keeping with the free play of his muscles as he walked. To-night there was something unusually restless in his movements, as he strode up and down, forgetting his wife's guests, conjuring possible futures, and trying to scratch characters on the blank sheets. He was young, he had a colossal fortune, he acknowledged no man's superiority, most paths were strewn with thorn-stripped roses at his approach, and yet, shortly after his thirty-sixth birthday, he walked solitary in a merry throng, wondering what he was to do with the rest of his life, lonely as any exile who passed his scintillating mansion with a rebellious oath.

He had started in life with many ideals. He wished to be a reformer, a wise and self-abnegating statesman, a friend of the people, a swayer of the thoughts of men. He knew no more of poverty in those days than any other Californian, but he was a student of political economy and a worshipper of Shelley. When at the age of twenty-two he found himself in unconditioned posses-

sion of his father's vast fortune he determined to
realize his ideals and that he might begin at the
root of politics ran at once for the Legislature of
his State. To his amazement and disgust he found
that he must buy his election as he bought his
horses and servants. If he finally consented to
"interview a boss" and negotiate for his victory
it was because he had come to the conclusion that
to accomplish a great deed some means must be
overlooked. It is needless to give the details of
his political career. It lasted five years and three
were passed in Washington. Then he withdrew,
disheartened, worn out with futile anger, his faith
in disinterested, single-purposed human nature
gone forever. He went to New York to stand
aghast before the raging sleepless epidemic for
wealth. Those everlasting monotonous rows of
brown-stone houses, eloquent of imagination
burned dry under the scorching breath of that
fever's sirocco, not a hand's width of grass before
them lest so many precious shekels should be lost!
"Money!" shrieked the flying trains as they
plunged into the crowded reeking districts of
squalor. "Money!" absently muttered the fur-

9

wrapped man on the hotel steps as he waited for
the bare-footed news-boy to give him change.
" Money!" sang the very air in endless echo.
Tremaine wrote a half dozen pamphlets and spent
a respectable fortune among the tenement wretches.
At the end of six months he questioned whether
he had done any good. No other rich man had
responded to his call, the funny-paragraphers had
paid their debts with his enthusiasms, and the poor
were as poor as ever. Once more determined to go
to the root of things, he crossed to England and
plunged into the thick of Socialism. He stayed
there two years. He attended every meeting of
importance and many whose doings were never
chronicled; he talked with every great reformer,
and allowed himself to be buttonholed by every
long-haired, illogical enthusiast who chose to spoil
the shape of his coat. He read all the literature
of the movement, calm, maniacal, practical, and
visionary. Then he left London as suddenly as
he had come. No man could tell him what was
wanted, for no man knew; nothing could be done
beyond talking and writing, for man's brain was
not yet hard enough and wide enough to solve the

problem. In the slow evolution of intelligence and
of events the question would be settled, but not
in his time. Sick at heart, surfeited to his finger-
tips with the unrelieved and aimlessly serious side
of life, he travelled madly for three years. He
walked every highway and rambled along many
a by-way; he lived books, and bit deep into the
apple of adventure. Then, weary of pleasure as
of significance, he returned to California and with
a flicker of expiring enthusiasm married the beautiful daughter of his father's partner. He dreamed
that he had found a phantasm he had pursued
even amid his zeal for universal welfare, and when
he awakened his rebellion for a short time was
deeper and more bitter than for all other shattered
ideals. But Life, harshly as she had used him,
had in compensation permitted him to drink
deeply at her fountain of Philosophy, and one day
he made up his mind to accept his fate without
further repining, took a vow that he would stand
by this last mad act as he had stood by all others
until they had turned from him and wear to the
end the consequences .he alone had contrived.
The world and his wife regarded him as a model

husband and he never crossed a whim of the woman who chilled his blood and heart. Sometimes his loneliness and hunger for human happiness leaped beyond bounds. Then he would shut himself among his books or throw himself on his organ stool, and in time a transient peace would come. As he grew older he turned from the future in a kind of terror. What was he to do with forty years of loveless life? Ambition was dead and he had no desire to revive and direct it to other tottering goals. He had known the walking embodiments of all talents, and the weary, selfish, disappointed, unsatisfactory races they ran, bred in him no desire to emulate. No, life and philosophy had taught him one great lesson—that personal happiness was the only good here below worth striving for. In all his contact with men he had never found one who was not pursuing it, however blindly, grandly, or contemptibly. The socialist strove for it in his attempt to adjust the world to that end, the minister of God clutched ever at it as he toiled to satisfy conscience and ideals, the politician intrigued for it as he sacrificed his fellow for place or power. And in this

little span why should a man waste his time seek-
ing for aught beside? If he let his neighbors
alone, harmed none, and gave when duty commanded, surely his list of responsibilities was
completed and he might paint the atmosphere of
this poor little life pink if he could. He would
but follow an instinct strong as that which makes
man man and woman woman, and with it towering above all others in the human organism.

His walk grew quicker and more restless. He
had solved the problem too late. There is small
comfort in unembodied philosophy; and never
had his future looked so blank and tasteless as it
looked to-night. It was as if he had come face to
face with it for the first time, as if a match had
been suddenly struck in some hitherto cobweb-
hung corridor in his brain. And those cobwebs
would never be spun again nor the lights go out.
He stopped with an angry gasp, and at the same
moment came an uncontrollable desire to get away
from his wife and all present conditions and go
straight to nature. His rare moments of happiness had been known in her solitudes. Should he
reserve that corner of the world he had just con-

quered, to fly to when spiritual suffocation was
threatening? His wife had other plans regarding
the Cerritos, but for once her will should yield to
his. If necessary he would buy her another
ranch—in a different part of California.

He turned impatiently as the rings of the por-
tière clanked together, but smiled as he saw the
keen good-natured face of the great journalist.

"Come in," he said hastily; "I am glad to see
you. I wondered if you were here."

"I have had a hunt for you," said the other,
"but I sympathize with your taste. With your
leave I will spend the rest of the evening in
here. This is the sort of room I like."

"Sit down, sit down," said Tremaine. He threw
himself into a deep chair, offered his guest a
cigar and they drifted into a discussion of current affairs. The journalist had known the
young man off and on for many years and had a
great liking for him. He admired his abilities
and in a measure understood his disappointments.
He had often wondered what he would make of
himself, and after the conversation with his wife
he felt that speculation must begin afresh.

"I hear that I am to congratulate you," he said at length. "Mrs. Tremaine tells me you have just won a most expensive and fatiguing law-suit."

"Yes; an abominably expensive and fatiguing one. They are an obstinate lot."

"What will you do now?"

"Well," said Tremaine, sliding downward in his chair until he was almost horizontal, and crossing his legs. "I hear that these people haven't much besides their huts, so if they want to buy or rent their farms on easy terms they can do so. I have written to my agent to that effect. I have some idea of building a big adobe house after old models and living in it occasionally. That portion of California which is comparatively untrodden is about as picturesque and satisfying as anything on this small globe. God! how small it is. And it has a personality (I can give it no other word) which makes it unique even in America. You feel as if some great incomprehensible yet most companionable force had singled out California and made it his home. Moreover, to be practical, the hunting and fishing ought to be very good on this ranch, and I think that with the addition of a library and an organ the Cerritos would be a highly livable place."

The journalist smiled, but sympathetically. " You do not appear to have discussed your plans with you wife."

"Oh, yes, she has talked of fitting it up on a grand scale and doing a lot of entertaining; but in reality the place would not suit her at all. She hates the country unless she can come to town in an hour, and she would find few people anxious for that trip. She has a house of her own at Menlo Park, and a lot of other houses to leave cards at, and one or two good roads where she can pass the same people every afternoon. In that fashionable suburb's placid monotony and soporific physiology she yawns back her roses and corresponds with her dressmaker. How I hate the place! It is the Sleepy Hollow of California. The Cerritos though! I wish you could see it. I'll take you down when my house is ready."

" I will devote a summer to its admiration; but —you don't mean to tell me that you are going to divide the rest of your life between fashionable society and a ranch? Get up and stir yourself.

You were born to some career. Go out and look
for it. Dig for it, if necessary."

"Damn careers," muttered his host; but he bit
through his cigar.

"Write a book and make yourself famous.
Fame compensates for a column of wants."

"O Fame!" said Tremaine impatiently. "Fame
that rescues a Jane Austen and passes an Emily
Brontë by! Fame that is oftener spelt with nine
letters than with four! Fame that is as kind to
cleverness as to genius! And in this era of all
eras it is the less worth while, for the world is
mad with its own sensationalism and knows not
the difference between the man who is striving to
be an artist, whether he succeed or not, and the
herd of cheap notorieties. I want none of it, if I
had the ability—which I have not. I have no talents; all I ask for is a life of action. I would
rather have one year of hard fighting than sit cross-
legged like a damned Turk in the Temple of
Fame for ten; but my lines have fallen in times
of peace——" He threw his cigar into the fire and
began striding up and down the room. His restlessness was growing beyond control and the mus-

cles of his erect powerful frame seemed to cast off vitality as he walked.

"Just now I am determined to have a change of some sort. I am as mad for a new experience as an unfledged college boy. And what is more it is coming. My experience of life has been that when one gets into that highly charged condition the experience is drawn as to a magnet. There is a long sight more of the unusual and romantic in life than is ever chronicled by the timid novelist. In fact the unexpected is about the one thing it is safe to bet on. What is this—a telegram?"

A Chinese servant in clinging silken robes was moving solemnly across the room, bearing a yellow envelope on a golden salver—the gift of a bonanza king.

"Pardon me," said Tremaine. He cast his eye over the telegram, then flung it on the table with an eager flash in the heavy blue of his eyes.

"It's from Hawkins—my Cerritos agent. He wires that the people refuse to rent, buy, or move. That not content with fighting the law they will now fight me. They have held mass-meetings, threatened to kill Hawkins—poor devil, how he

must be shaking in his boots; he is able but not
courageous—and swear they will never move a
yard from their mud hovels. Hawkins says that
he has wired to the nearest town for the sheriff
and deputies, but I shall go down myself. Here
is the experience, you see. How I should enjoy
one or two hand-to-hand fights with some brawny
Mexican! The very thought stimulates me.
Come; let us go and have a glass of champagne.
You can come back here after, if you like."

"By Jove, you have got the restlessness of
California in you," said the journalist as he rose,
nothing loath, to follow his host. "You'll burn
out in about ten years."

*   *   *   *   *   *

The dining-room was the pride of Mrs. Tremaine's artistic brain. The walls were hung with
tapestries whose every rotting thread was price-
less. The old oaken sideboards and mantel had
been brought from Venice, and built into walls of
a wood whose parent tree had not been felled
when the knife had carved these alien grafts.
Heavy beams barred the ceiling, gold and crystal
glittered on the old banquetting table, the sweet-

meats were triumphs of national art. Banks of
flowers rounded the corners of the room, and the
fanciful china between thé Venetian columns
gleamed through yellow roses and purple violets.
The massive chairs were worthier of biographies
than most men, and the floor was a mosaic repre-
senting a redwood. Somebody was once startled
into an unhappy exclamation at this last daring
incongruity, but Mrs. Tremaine snubbed him into
silence by suavely remarking that the redwoods
where older than either the tapestries or the chairs.

The room was crowded, and champagne lay like
amber pools in little crystal basins. As Tremaine
entered each guest raised his sparkling glass.

"Here's to your continued good luck," cried the
lawyer who had won the famous suit. "We all
congratulate you."

PART II.

THE MAN.

I.

THE DAUGHTER OF JOAQUIN MURIETTA.

IN Castro's field an immense bonfire blazed, reddening the sky like an angry volcano, and throwing into fitful black-shadowed relief the hills on
the other side of the river. The watch fire had not
beckoned in vain and a small army of men were
gathered about a table whereon stood the master-
spirit of the Cerritos Rancho.

Castro was shouting rebellion with clashing
teeth and savage gestures. His great hairy chest
was bare, and his purple, scowling face and thun-
dering voice were enough in themselves to frighten
his subjects into submission. The men interrupted
him with frequent cheers of approval, and as they
surged excitedly about in the red dancing light
they looked like a horde of rioting demons.

" Oh we no going," he roared. " We are three
hundred mens and boys, and we have knives and
bullets yet. The sheriffs coming to-morrow?

Letting them!" (With a terrible volley of oaths.)
"We washing them in their own blood and throw
them in the river to fat the fish. Who farming
this land? Who builda the houses? The Señor
Alejandro Tremaine?—black diablo how he is!
No! we doing it and it is ours. I maka this field
grow wheat where are nettles before. I cutta the
treeses and maka that fence. I digga the earth
and maka my house. I giva my muscles, my
times, my sense. The Señor Tremaine can he taka
that? Can he taka the years of my life I putting here? Then si he no can taka those, he no
can taka whatte they make, for the two maka one.
Si the Señor Tremaine *need*, that make another
thing. But he no need; he have so much he no
knowing whatte to do with all. Si we keeping our
homes he no starve; he no knowing the differ-
encia. No! fighting! fighting! fighting! Throwing him on the ground! Spit on him! Hang him
to a tree and filling him with buck-shot! Stay in
your housses with your guns at your windows;
he no can take si you no give. He and all the
damned white-liver agents and sheriffs go to run
like the rabbits when they seeing us come."

He leaped from the table amidst loud-voiced excitement; but it was evident that some difference of opinion existed in the audience. In a moment Espinoza was hoisted upon the table and a respectful silence fell at once.

"There no mus be blood," he said. "The Señor Tremaine he no knowing, perhaps, whatte he do; the rich man, he lova the money and the land; he no meaning be cruelle. For that we mus have be careful and no losta our souls to send his to hell; for si he live and be old he may bimeby feel sorry. But for the other—Castro, he is right. The housses are ours and we no going, si we can help. We are three hundred and we can maka the sheriffs run, and bimeby the Señor feel tire out and letting us stay. And si he come himself and see the childrens, he no turning them out. But no fire the gun and no usa the knife."

The speech was received with mingled murmurs of disapproval and assenting cheers, and the moment was a critical one. Castro, trembling for his supremacy, was about to raise his voice again when a new figure suddenly appeared on the table. It was a woman this time and as startling in her

10

way as Castro had been in his. Her loose black hair, caught by the wind, swept to and fro behind her head like an ominous cloud, her eyes seemed to reflect the intense, angry brilliancy of the reddened stars, and in the scarlet glare of the ever-leaping fire she looked as if about to disappear above the tree-tops in a chariot of flame.

"Carmelita! Carmelita!" cried Castro ecstatically. "Letting her spik. Listen to her and no say one word. No one word!"

Before the astonished silence had time to fall Carmelita's far-carrying voice was sounding through the field, rising high above the roar of the river and the crackling of the flames.

"Yes! Yes! Kill him!" she cried, carried out of her womanhood by the weirdness of the scene and the terrible wrongs which had dragged the fierce nature of her father from the depths where it ever lightly slept. "Si he go to take our housses, kill him, for it is right. Think of the childrens—they have no one dress, some of them, and the weather so cold. Where they sleep? In the wet field, where they die in a week? Think of your wives who go to have the babies, and of those who nurse the others! And think how they work for you, and how they cry and scream when they see the babies die and they no can help! And the old womens who sit in the sun and shake with the age. Mus they sleep with the pigs and the sheep, and hug them to keep warm on the wet ground when the wind moan?" She paused for a moment and then leaned forward with her arms outstretched. "And you know," she went on, her voice growing hoarse with rage—"you know how the man who take our homes, he live? He have a house big like Castro's field. The carpets thick on the floors like the violet beds in the forest, and all your crops for ten years no could buy one. The glass in the windows one big thick shining sheet like the springs under the rocks, and the curtains like spring clouds that have catch in them the maiden-hair that grow on the cliffs. He have pianos that sing like birds, but were make from trees that now can be the homes of the birds no more; and chairs so soft that si you sit in one, you no work any more. And the beds—you think they are like yours, make of boards and straw that scratch? No! they are make from the feath-

ers of chickens and geese—thousands and millions
—when we no can get one to lay the egg! And
you think they eat in the one room? No—they
have one sala big like your whole house, and they
eat little birds off plates of gold, and drink yellow
whiskey out of cups o' glass that shine like the
stars. And the wife de that man what put us out?
You think she wear rags like your wives, and no
have shawl in the winter? Oh, no! when it is
cold she wear the dress like the thick green moss
on the trees, and what they call furs that are like
the wool on the bear. And when it is warm she
dress like the flowers, and drive in a wagon, big
like the stage, with gold harness, and pillows make
from the skin of the cow who no give us milk.
And *he* "—she threw back her body, and raised her
arm, looking like a prophetess inspired by heaven
to foretell the doom of nations. " And *he*—he sit
on a throne of gold like God in the picture in the
Mission, and say to the lawyer, 'My cellars are
full de gold. Go helpa yourself and turn the mens
from their housses and take their farms that the
childrens can starve. I no want the land for more
bread; I have whole towns and many ranchos

now, but I no know what to do with my moneys,
so the poor man mus die. And I love to think
that bimeby I have more moneys still from those
farms and those trees so I can buy another rancho
and turn out more childrens to sleep in the fields
and scream with the rheumatismo in their little
joints. Oh! Lopez, Diaz, Jamova, Verela, and you
Clarke and H nter and Miller with your little
cotton-haired children,—tear this man in pieces
si he no give you your housses. He no is fit to
live, and Hell no can wait for him longer."

Exhausted as much by the bound her imagination had taken as by the strain on her throat,
Carmelita dropped suddenly from the table into
Castro's arms. Her strength returned at his touch,
and she wrenched herself free, spurning him from
her. But he flung himself on his knees at her
feet, biting her hands in the savageness of his
caress, and tearing her skirt from its gathers.

"Carmelita! Carmelita!" he gasped, his hoarse
voice almost inaudible, "I roasta the world in hell
si you give me one kiss. Throwa me down, stamp
on me like the wild cows tramp the sheeps, I
scream with joy, for you toucha me. I go to San

Francisco and killing this man, si you say. You no can say do it one thing I no do. O Carmella, Carmella mia! I tear God from his throne and putting you there, si you only say, 'Castro, I marrying you! I loving you!'"

Carmelita, panting and horrified at the terrible ardor of the brute and at the touch of his thick hot lips, tore herself from his clutching fingers and flew over the field, unheeding the shouts of admiration that followed her. Castro made no attempt at pursuit; he knew that every man in the field would fly to her protection if he did; but taking advantage of the impression her words had made, he sprang upon the table and poured forth a wild and blasphemous speech which wrought the squatters up to the pitch of madness and routed the pacifie council of Espinoza into oblivion.

II.

TWO CONFESSIONS.

WHEN Carmelita reached home she fell on her bed. Faint and cold-veined through reaction, she lay and thought with horror on what she had done. Suppose those men should kill Tremaine and go to the gallows with murder on their souls? Who would have sent them there? What devil had prompted her to spring upon the table and excite the passions of the men at a time when they most needed calm? But the hot flood of rage and despair and hatred that had been rising in her heart during all these bitter months had suddenly boiled over its crater like lava when Nature is in her angry moods. And Castro! That beast to have touched her! She had a hot sense of having been defiled, and she got up suddenly and thrust her hands above their wrists into a gourd of water, then went back to bed and sobbed herself to sleep, only to wake again and again.

The next morning she had a headache for the first time in her life and was inclined to think that retribution had come and she was going to die. But after strolling about in the open air for a time she felt better and concluded to confess her sins of the night before to the padre and consult him in regard to the certificate.

When she arrived at his house he was not there, and she amused herself cooking his dinner. He came in shortly after noon and his tired face lightened when he saw her.

"I am glad to see you, mi Carmella," he said patting her head. " You are so inextricably a part of my life on this ranch that I cannot believe in your going, and your presence cheers me."

"Oh, padre mio," faltered the girl. "I have done so terreeblay a thing."

He smiled. " Have you forgotten your rosary again?—or stolen the mustang? "

"Mi padre, it is worse, more worse than that," and without giving her courage time to ebb she gave a repentant account of her maiden speech.

He looked grave as he listened. "But she is right," he muttered to himself, "she is right."

"It is impossible to tell what the consequences will be," he said aloud, when she had finished, "but I don't believe they will be as bad as you think. With the exception of Castro and one or two others, the squatters are not inclined to be murderous. The Mexicans are sullen and the Americans desperate and indignant, but in the main, sensible. They will hold their farms until the last minute, and perhaps attempt to cow the sheriffs, but I don't think they will shed blood. In the average brain is planted a wholesome regard for the law, and the sheriffs will win the fight and keep their blood in the bargain."

"And we going?" cried Carmelita.

The priest shook his head sadly. "My dear girl, I am afraid you must. Even if you fought to the death, the sheriff at any moment could summon the militia and sweep you all down like grass before the mower."

"And what we do? There no is one acre de Government land for forty miles. The wagons are in pieces, and we no have enough si they were good. How the childrens walk forty miles, and the poor womens?"

"Lightfoot has said that you can camp on his ranch for the present, and the women and children can stay there while the men go ahead and prepare homes for them. I will see that they do not starve, and when the men return for them I will go to all the neighboring ranchos and take up a collection for their transportation by stage."

Carmelita sat down by the hearth and buried her face in her lap. Never before had she felt that the case was so utterly hopeless. She lifted her head in a few moments. "Bueno," she said sullenly. "Si we go, we go. But," and the demon awoke once more, "the Señor Tremaine I hope he die with no one crust to eat, and si he have childrens I hope he see their bones come through the skins."

"Carmelita!" exclaimed the padre, mindful of his calling.

She took the certificate from her dress. "I find this in the Mission. What I can do with it to make the money?"

The padre lifted his brows as he read the bit of paper. "This thing certainly has its value," he said, "it is very old and is signed with a famous name. But who on this place would buy it?"

"I think I ask Tio Pedro to give to the stage driver. He can sell in the town."

He shook his head. "No one in the small towns would know its value. You would not get a dime for it and the driver would probably lose——"

"I know," exclaimed Carmelita, with a sudden inspiration. "I give to Geraldine and she—— Padre mio! what is the matter?"

The priest had thrown himself forward and grasped her arm, his dark face almost black.

"What name did you say?" he demanded hoarsely, his grip tightening on her arm.

Carmelita sank back in consternation. "Oh, I forget! I forget!" she cried. "I promise never to say her name."

"Whose name?" he shook her arm roughly. "Tell me at once."

She looked at him; obedience to the padre had been a pleasant duty, but it was a fixed habit, nevertheless.

"The señora at Lindavista."

"Ah! that woman who is never seen. Tell me what she is like." His lips were quivering now, his eyes dilating.

But at this point Carmelita rebelled. "No,"
she said, "I no do that. I say to her I never will,
and I no will, even to you, padre."

"Tell me," he cried harshly as if he had not
heard, "are her eyes green and is her hair yellow?
Is her skin white and her lips red——" He saw
the answer in the girl's startled eyes, and springing to his feet he paced up and down the narrow
room. Suddenly striding over to Carmelita he
caught her by the shoulder and raising her to her
feet pushed her to the door. "Go! Go!" he
muttered. "Leave me. I must be alone."

And terrified by what she saw in his face Carmelita fled from the house.

She went directly to Geraldine, partly to confess her breach of trust, partly to ask her to dis-
pose of the certificate. When she reached Lindavista she found her friend lying on the divan with
a cologne-soaked handkerchief on her head. Geraldine had grown older during the last year.
There were violet shadows under her eyes and the
mouth was drawn. She held out her hand with a
smile—almost of gratitude.

"I am so glad you have come. I have heard of

your speech last night. You are a wonderful girl; but happy you will be if you never see that life of the world. How flat you would find it! But—there is no fresh trouble?"

Carmelita sat down on the floor and leaned her head against the divan. She found her second confession much harder than her first. *Would* she be forgiven?

"O Geraldina," she began, "I have something terreeblay to say."

The woman's face turned a shade paler. "What is the matter?" she asked faintly.

"Oh, how I can say it? Geraldina, what you think I do? I say your name to the padre!"

Geraldine sat upright, as if some one had suddenly lifted her. "And what did he say? What did he do?" she demanded, the words tumbling one over the other.

Carmelita gave a graphic account of what the priest had said and done. She felt as if she were being torn in twain that day, but her sympathies were too keenly with the woman to deny her request. Geraldine listened, the blood rising to her hair, then sweeping back to her heart until she gasped for breath. When the girl had finished she dropped back on the pillows and turning on her side hid her face. But feminine curiosity had by this time taken triumphant possession of Carmelita. She raised herself to her knees and laid her head caressingly on her friend's shoulder.

"Tell me, querida," she said coaxingly, "what you know by the padre before you come here?"

Geraldine shook from head to foot, and then burst into heavy dry-eyed sobs. Carmelita put both arms around her and cried in sympathy, yet with that exquisite sensation which a woman ever feels when about to lift the curtain of a love affair in which the element of mystery is dominant.

Geraldine turned and pressed her head against the girl's shoulder. When the paroxysm had passed she lay without speaking for a few moments, panting a little.

"Tell me," whispered Carmelita, whose patience was ebbing.

"I cannot tell you all, dearest. Only this much: I knew your padre once—and loved him. And— why should I deny it?—I love him still. It is for him I have left the world—that I might be near

him, even if I never saw him. But now that he
knows I am here I suppose I must go."

"No, no," cried Carmelita. "You no go and leave
me. The padre no is sure it is you and I never tell
him, never! never!"

"Oh! but he does know it is I. And now that
I know he knows, it will not be so easy to keep
silence. Already that passive endurance to which
I have schooled myself during the past year is
gone and I feel eager for something to happen—
for the climax to come. But if he had never
known I could have gone on forever."

"Would you have stay here alway?"

"Yes, until I died or he went away. Then I
would have followed him."

Carmelita smoothed the yellow hair that was
falling over her shoulder. "Pobre Geraldinita!
But he suffer too. I know that. Always, even
when I am a little girl, I know he no is happy."

The hand which clasped Carmelita's gave it a
closer pressure.

"You no are angry with me?"

"No. I would not have had you tell him, but
now that it is done I am almost—glad."

She rose and went into the next room. When she returned her face was calm and she sat down before Carmelita. " Now tell me of your own affairs," she commanded. " Have you heard anything further? "

Carmelita shook her head despondently, but produced the certificate. " Perhaps you know of some one who buy that? " she said.

"Ah! " exclaimed Geraldine, as she read the paper, " I can get you money for this. I have a friend in San Francisco who has a mania for such things and I will send it to him at once. You ought to get a twenty-dollar gold piece at least."

Carmelita opened her eyes, " Dio mio! " she gasped, " I buy closes for all the childrens and a bag of beans." Then she rose, divining that Geraldine wished to be left alone.

"Adios, mijita," she said. " I mus go, now. I come again, for we no go yet."

Geraldine opened the door for her and kissed her good-by, then turned the key and sank to the floor clutching the curtain in her convulsive hands, but uttering no sound.

III.

INCARNATE.

CARMELITA walked slowly homeward, her mind crowded with an army of thoughts—those led by Geraldine and those by the squatters fighting for supremacy. What had Geraldine been to the padre? It was none of her affair, but she did wish that she knew. It was the most romantic incident which had entered her life; the loves and woes of the birds paled before it. *She* would never have a sorrow like that. Her troubles were all of the sordid kind; to sit by and weep fiercely while the children starved, or moaned with the cold; or to feel the wolf gnawing at her own vitals, and won-der where her next dress was to come from; it would be made of bean bags, most likely.

She stood still with a feeling of surprise. She had the same sensation, half eager, half restful, which always touched her when she approached her redwood. But he was not near her to-day;

11

he was high on the mountain with the spring-flowers at his feet. She looked behind her. Far away shimmered the mountain like a dark blue tidal wave which had caught a forest in its rush. Between, were a hundred green hills spangled with flowers. The air was mad with melody and in-toxicating with perfume. The sun sent waves of delicious warmth to the very hearts of the joyous flowers. The earth lay wrapped in her newly woven garment, sensuous and dreamy. Slowly, involuntarily, Carmelita turned. A man stood at the bend of the road.

She made a quick unreasoning step toward him, then drew back and put her hand to her eyes. She felt as if the earth were swaying with the gen-tle movement of a cradle, as if the unseen stars had swept downward and were pelting her like golden hail. Then she felt a sudden sensation of pain and she wondered vaguely if it were for Ger-aldine—or if she had forgotten her.

"What is it?" asked Tremaine gently. "You are not ill?" And he thought as he spoke that he had never seen so beautiful a woman.

His commonplace words and a strong feminine

instinct combined to restore her self-control. " Si,
señor," she said, almost coldly, " I am no very
well for to-day," and she moved down the road.

" You look the picture of health," he said aimlessly, as he walked beside her; " but although the
weather is much warmer are not you cold in that
thin dress? "

Carmelita threw back her head, stung by the
commiseration in his voice. " It is the same I
wear alway," she replied haughtily. " I am use
to it." She look askance at him. He wore gray
travelling clothes and a soft felt hat. *What* was
he? She had never seen any one with whom to
compare him. And he was so tall and strong.
Could trees assume the form of men again and
walk the earth? She glanced over her shoulder
once more at the mountain; but that vaporous
ocean told no tales.

"And who is she? " thought Tremaine. " Probably the daughter of one of these squatters. But
she might be a young goddess. Will you tell
me your name? " he asked aloud.

" Carmelita Murietta."

"And you live here on the Cerritos Rancho? "

She laughed shortly. His words recalled the prosaic miseries of life and wafted other sensa-tions to dreamland. "Yes, I live here to-day, but to-morrow, perhaps, I live in the grass of the Col-minares Raucho. The Señor Tremaine say we go, so we go, I suppose. But we fight! we fight!"

Tremaine felt rather awkward. Was he actu-ally taking the roof from this glorious creature's head? It was true that she was a goddess and should lie in beds of poppies with the clouds for curtains, but probably she was not used to sleep-ing out of doors and didn't like it.

"And so you are one of the squatters who must go?" he said lamely. "I am very sorry."

She laughed again. "Yes, you are more sorry si you see the childrens who no have shirt to the back or beans in the stomach. We have a little lef now, and a few sheeps, but soon we have noth-ing. Oh, the Señor Tremaine! how I hate him! Señor, he have gold enough to fill the hill there, si it was holla out, and he turn us out our haci-endas and leave us to starve."

Tremaine grew hot to his hair, but although he had braved the wrath of the squatters he had not the courage to reveal himself to this girl. How could he reason with her? He knew how futile all words must be, but he felt impelled to right himself if he could.

"But, señorita, the squatters knew for a year that the ranch was not theirs. They had plenty of time to find homes elsewhere before they spent all their money on a law-suit. And if Mr. Tremaine paid a large price for this ranch —as he undoubtedly did—it surely is his. That is only common reason."

"It no is his," cried Carmelita indignantly. She was not to be deceived by the sophistries of men. "It is ours. We have it first, and the land was make so the poor man can live, not for the rich man to buy cause he no know what to do with his moneys. The Señor Tremaine no is better make than us. Why then he have millions and we starve? Why he have the great house in San Francisco and take our haciendas from us? No man have the right to say to other man, 'Go starve. I have plenty but I no care.' When Adam and Eve are born they only are give one garden and they are the only peoples on the earth. But God

—who talk to peoples in those days; now he have so many he no can—he no let them take more. He say: 'No, you no can have more than you need. Leave the other for those who come bime by, that all may be well and happy, like the birds' (who never take what no is theirs, nor want). But Eve she eat the apple, and Satan tell her children to take one from the other and keep his own."

"Well! well!" exclaimed Tremaine, "that is the most original interpretation of the Bible I have heard yet. Will you sit down here?"

They had reached the Mission and Carmelita was not sorry to take possession of a box and lean against the wall. Tremaine sat beside her and watched her furtively. He had not been so interested in a woman for years. She must have sprung from the earth like the great red poppies over yonder. He would not believe that she was of mortal parentage. He wondered if she ever bent a bow. If he were a painter he would put her in a picture as Diana.

Carmelita had thrust her restive womanhood under and bolted a trap-door above it, but she made no attempt to stifle the frankness and confidence

the stranger inspired. That he was Tremaine never
occurred to her. She had long since made up her
mind that the hated tyrant was a little dried-up
old man with the sardonic features, not to say the
cloven hoof, of the devil. What this man's name
was she did not even wish to know.

Tremaine looked at her with a smile. He had
a very charming smile, half-indulgent, half-sym-
pathetic, and the more effective in that the gaze
which accompanied it was usually very long and
direct, as if he found it hard to remove his eyes.

" That is good reasoning though, especially for a
woman," he added teasingly. " But the question
has often arisen in my mind—you will understand,
of course, that there is nothing personal in this;
I know nothing of the people here—whether the
great number of the lower classes are worth doing
anything for; whether the world would not be
better if a good many of them were out of it. I
have often thought that a discriminating plague
would solve the problem better than all the rant-
ing of the socialists. Do you understand—those
who were left would have more elbow-room and a
surer chance to rise."

"What!" cried Carmelita with flashing eyes. "I no believe one word that. Si people no are of use in the world why they are born? They no come cause they want; they come cause they no can help. What good you are in the world?" She put the question with a struggle; but her wrongs were deep and always mastered her.

He laughed somewhat bitterly. " Really, señorita, none."

" You have plenty moneys?"

"Yes; a good deal."

"And what you do with it?"

" Well, I travel a good deal," he said, now highly amused, "and I buy books and beautiful things. Altogether I get out of life about as much as there is in it."

"And you never give to the poor peoples?"

" O yes. I give certain regular sums to certain charitable institutions and I generally give the newsboys and flower-girls a dinner at Christmas."

"Well, you no are so bad," admitted Carmelita. " Have you the land?"

" Yes—some."

"And what you do with it?"

" Well, I rent it usually to farmers, or cattle-raisers. Both pay very well."

"And you make the poor man pay rent when you have the moneys to do all what you want?" This with deep indignation.

" But, my dear señorita, I would not have the money for all that I want if my land did not yield me an income. If my land were not rented what good would it do me?"

"And you think you are more of importance than the hundred, two, three hundred farmers who rent your land?" cried Carmelita fiercely. " You think it is right that the poor man who work all the day give you half what he make so you can go to the great cities and buy the books? Si you do that I think you are very bad man."

" Upon my word, you make me feel like a thief. But will you allow me this much defence: I am not responsible for the existing order of things. I did not draw the social diagram nor plant the lawns of prosperity and the vegetable garden of poverty. Both are somewhat time-honored insti-tutions and I am but a child of circumstances. In plainer language I cannot help the way things are, and I but follow the lead of the world."

"Caramba!" she exclaimed, "that is the more foolish thing I hear you say yet. The padre he say it is the custom in the world to say no true. That make it right for me to say no true? The bad mens down here have the custom to steal the horses from the big ranchos. That make it right for my uncle to take Miller's horse? No. Si half the world buy all the land and keep the poor out, it no is more right than si only one man do it. What is right *is* right. Custom no can change."

"I cannot reason with this girl," thought Tremaine, "she is too keen and too ignorant. If I should tell her that custom does change things, she would merely laugh me to scorn. And if I should tell her that I once made a fool of myself and spent more money than she could count, trying to adjust a world that had baffled wiser heads, she would simply tell me to go back and peg away until I made off to a world where, let us devoutly hope, each man lives in a golden hut and political economy is an unknown science. But I should like to talk to her all day. "What is that?" he

demanded abruptly. The bell of the Mission was
tolling above him.

"It is the vesper. We only have it once in the
week now. The peoples they no can come more
often—once they feel like coming!"

Tremaine looked over his shoulder through the
door of the church. "Have you an organ?" he
asked hesitatingly.

Carmelita leaned forward eagerly. "You—oh,
you make the musica? Si, we have one or-*gan*.
The padre he buy and the school-ma'am she play
for the mass. But for the vesper she no come;
and she no play like they play in the city, the
padre, he say. O señor, play, si you can. I so
much want to hear the musica re-al."

"You are sure your padre would not object?"

"He like! He love the musica. For that he
buy the or-*gan*."

"Very well. I rely upon you to make my peace
with him." He followed Carmelita into the Mission and went up the rude steps to the little organ platform. The women, with shawls pinned
over their heads, came in one by one, dropped on
their knees and crossed themselves; the padre,

entering from the sacristy, made the sign of the cross and knelt before the altar; Tremaine began to play softly. His fingers grasped the keys as if they were living things that he loved, and he held them as if he would draw the sound from the organ's soul and imprison it in his own. Carmelita listened breathlessly, ecstatically, every fibre of her nature vibrating in unison. Even the voice of the padre grew fuller and more inspired.

Tremaine played throughout the short service, and gazed absently upon the rude religious scene about him with a vague feeling that it was one of a coming series of pictures he should never forget. The windows were gone from the time-battered old Mission, the plaster peeled from its walls, the earthen floor was sinking above the buried priests, forlornly huddled the saints on the altar. Then through the melancholy casements came a flood of golden sunset, and for a few brief moments the Mission was triumphant in splendor. Even the coarse outlines and hard care-worn faces of the few kneeling worshippers were glorified into a short unreal beauty like that given by a halo to the commonplace head of a saint. The low rich notes of the organ throbbed through the inarticulate sound of prayer and the voice of the priest as he intoned the psalms; but without, the world might have sunk to eternal rest, it was so quiet.

The padre turned to his people and made the sign of the cross, then withdrew as he had come; the women stumbled to their feet and passed out, staring with drowsy curiosity at the unaccustomed organist, but Carmelita remained on her knees, spell-bound. Then Tremaine struck the keys with imperious fingers and a Gregorian chant pealed through the Mission, filling it from end to end. Carmelita listened, quivering from head to foot, then suddenly sprang to her feet, and rushing from the church, flew over the hills to her home.

IV.

NATURE AWAKENS.

TREMAINE had arrived at the Aguitas at mid-
night to find that Hawkins had heralded him as
his friend, Mr. Smith.

" You must keep dark till the sheriffs turn up,"
he explained as he hustled Tremaine into his room.
"These squatters'd as soon kill yer as look at yer.
I know you ain't afraid of nothin'," in reply to
Tremaine's impatient protest, "but yer'd jest be a
fool, nothin' morn less, if yer went passearin'
around this blazin' ranch in yer own name before
the sheriffs come, and I don't spose yer want to
be cooped up in this hole."

" When are the sheriffs expected?"

"Not for two or three days. They're after a
murderer and they can't come here till they've
run him down. Now be reasonable, Mister Tremaine. It wouldn't be bravery, it ud jest be
damned tomfoolery."

Tremaine slept on the proposition and concluded that his prudent servitor was right. He wanted a few days of solitude and aimless wandering, and he had no desire to take either, pistol in hand. He always experienced a sense of freedom and of infinite possibilities when in the wilds of California that he never felt elsewhere, and he had a mighty desire to get out of himself once more. The interval before the sheriffs' coming was brief, but it was something, and then—the more excitement the better.

The day after his first interview with Carmelita he met her again as he was riding along the river-bank, fishing-pole in hand. She turned from him in a sort of blind terror. All night she had lain face downward on her bed, refusing to think, but hearing always vast harmonies, peals of melody, which ever and anon broke into shrieking discords. Once or twice she had half sprung from the bed, the blind instinct of the animal for its mate moving restlessly in its sleep beneath her heart.

"I was hoping to meet you," cried Tremaine. "I am sure you can tell me where to find some good fishing. I see nothing here."

His direct matter-of-fact words broke the spell of the night.

" In the creek on the mountain are plenty feesh," she said. " I see them often."

" So I have heard. But I do not know the way. Won't you be good enough to show me? " He had suddenly lost his desire for solitude.

" It is there," pointing to the olive mountains.

" But, señorita, that is a mountain forest and I am sure the creek does not run around the outside of it. Please come with me."

Carmelita hesitated. " Bueno," she said at last. " Wait here till I come."

She was but a short distance from her uncle's hacienda and returned in a few moments on the unprincipled mustang. Tremaine could not repress a smile as she approached him. She bestrode the animal as unconcernedly as a lad and dug her little bare heels into its flanks. The red collar of her blouse fell away from her strong brown throat and her position pulled the short skirt to her knees. " She was never born for clothes at all," Tremaine thought; " she might be the primitive woman."

Carmelita led the way across the narrow bridge, then, raising her bridle, started off on a mild canter. She was not inclined to be talkative, and Tremaine, after two or three futile attempts to draw her out, gave it up and consoled himself with the beauty of the day. A week of warm weather, which had come like a wave straight from the inner chambers of the sun, had ripened the country into a glory of color. Beds of pale blue baby-eyes bordered hillocks of red and yellow poppies, and between the groves of moss-draped trees were miniature forests of gold and purple lupins. The grain was waving in the fields, and the gophers, whistling, sped through the grass.

"There is no more lovely spot in California, or anywhere else, for that matter," exclaimed Tremaine enthusiastically. "I could never tire of it, and I am sure you never have."

"No," said Carmelita, her eyes filling with tears and turning her head away, "I never tire."

"*You* shall not go," he exclaimed impulsively; and as she turned to him in surprise, "I know this man, Tremaine, and have some influence with

12

him. I am sure I can persuade him to let you keep your farm."

She raised her head proudly. "Si all go, I go. Si he give to all because it is right, I stay; but I no take from him like a favor."

"What a combination she is!" he thought, "she makes other women seem like dolls." Aloud he said, "But would you not stay for your uncle's sake? He surely does not want to go."

"My uncle no would stay si the others go."

"Not for the sake of his wife and children?"

Her pride showed signs of weakening. "I no know. It is hard to hear the childrens cry for the food and for the closes to keep warm."

"But surely you have never heard that. This seems to be the land of plenty."

She laughed bitterly. "It no was the land of plenty this winter, señor. We have give all the moneys to the lawyers and no have much left to buy the beans and the flour. And it was very cold, señor, and rain, rain, rain. Three or four childrens die by the lungs. Si we no have the padre and the señora I think we starve."

"It isn't possible!" exclaimed Tremaine. "Are you as poor as that?"

"O señor, we are very poor!"

"Great heaven!" he thought, "I will give these people the price of their crops. No wonder they made a row, poor devils. I shall certainly speak to Tremaine," he said, "and I know he will do something for these men."

"Oh, he no will!" cried the girl. "He is a perfec devil. He have a heart black like the earth the gopher over there turn up, but hard like the stones in the creek."

Tremaine felt much as if his ears had been boxed.

"But perhaps he did not understand," he expostulated, "when I explain matters to him I am sure he will do all he can to compensate you."

Then he experienced a strong desire to change the conversation. There should be no clouds on so perfect a day, and he might never have this girl alone again. "By the way," he said abruptly, "is there a Mrs. Pollock staying in the neighborhood—on any of these ranches?"

Carmelita shook her head. "Who she is?"

"She is a woman who was once a great belle in

San Francisco. There was a rumor of an unfortunate affair, which you would not understand, señorita, and she suddenly disappeared. It was supposed at first that she had gone abroad again, but of late it has come to be generally understood that she is living on a ranch in Central California."

Carmelita caught her breath. Could he mean Geraldine? But her loyalty was stronger than her curiosity. She raised her hand and pointed to the mountains they were approaching.

"Mira," she said.

The soft olive curtain had slowly lifted and the mountain no longer looked like a mirage. The redwoods stood out boldly against the darkening aisles, and the wind rising, sighed a welcome through the pines.

Tremaine's lids fell lower. The world was still, but he felt the litany of the redwoods. Nature laid her heart against his own and stilled its discontent. Carmelita, with rapt eyes, made the sign of the cross, and he felt her kinship. If there had been even less of common language between them he would at that moment have divined the comrade in her as absolutely and uniquely as if they had whispered confidences from the hour of birth.

She did not take him up the mountain by her usual trail, but by one rougher, more precipitous, and a mile beyond.

"Better we tie the horses here, so they no feel tire out," she said after they had climbed about a quarter of a mile. "You can walk the rest of the way, no? It no is very far."

Tremaine dismounted, glad to be on his legs again. He turned to help Carmelita, but she was already on the ground tethering her mustang. She sprang as lightly as a squirrel up the steep trail, but paused after a time to await Tremaine, who was following with less agility.

"Now we go through the brush," she called down to him. "I hope you no tear your closes."

He stopped suddenly and looked up at her. She was several yards above him, standing on a sort of shelf that projected over the path. Behind was a dense mass of green and above her towered the redwoods. Her hands rested lightly on her splendid young hips and her head was a little thrown back. The round elastic form looked as if it might bound away into the forest like a deer, and her great eyes seemed guarding the mystery of the forest's infancy, locked in their depths.

He went up the path, as usual saying what was second in his mind.

"I am not afraid of the brush."

She looked at the clothes he wore, then at the redwoods. "They are gray like the trees," she said; "sometime I think you are a redwood before," and then she dashed into the willows.

Tremaine put his hat in the pocket of his fishing jacket and holding his rod in one hand, forced back the boughs with the other. Conversation was not to be thought of here. The slender, rebounding branches switched his face as if he were a disobedient school-boy, the wild-rose trees caught at his trousers, and the lilacs, sweet as they were, filled his eyes with a blinding shower. He emerged upon the bluff overhanging the creek, with a sigh of relief.

"Thank heaven that is over," he exclaimed fervently. "Do you come here often?"

"No by this way. I have another more open."

"Then why—why did you bring me this way?"

" I have reason," said Carmelita, and Tremaine, quite snubbed, put on his hat and followed her down the bluff.

" Have be careful," she said, " the earth is loose."

Slipping, sliding, and catching at shrubs, they reached the creek. Carmelita waded out into the middle, then turned to Tremaine.

" You mus come in," she said. " You no can catch on the bank. It no is deep enough there. Oh! I forget. You mus take off your shoses and stockings—no put on the boots."

" They are rubber boots," he said, and followed his guide into the water.

" When you see the feesh you stand on the rocks and throw out the line," she said, " I hold the basket for you. There one is now."

He mounted the slippery rocks, whipped the stream and his first fish swung slowly to Camelita, who stood on a big stone near by.

" Bueno! " she said approvingly. " Now come after me and have be careful for the sharp stones."

They plodded up the stream for an hour, Tremaine catching a number of fine trout. It was very beautiful, very cool, and very quiet. Noth-

ing could be wilder or more picturesque, nothing
more calmly eloquent of the gulf between nature
and art. Great bunches of ice-grass with their
slender sweeping strands reflected in the gliding
waters; banks of ferns, thick and strong as young
forests, or delicate as lace for a woman's gown;
gnarled and twisted roots of trees, some massive,
others in their first cycle, crawling in and out of
the steep sides of the bluffs like writhing living
things, side by side with fresh vivid patches of
wet moss or an occasional oak that stretched out
at right angles from the cliff; sloping banks hidden beneath dense beds of feathery fox-tail and
gay pageant of lilies; wild fragrant honeysuckles,
and masses of pink azaleas; sweeping willows and
crisp laurel; and high above, the mountain with
its silent redwoods and bending pines. In the
creek were dim tideless pools and tiny white-
tipped tumbling falls. Side by side were many-
hued rocks and great logs, now covered, now
rearing their heads like watchful crocodiles. The
winding sweep was lost in darkening sun-flecked
cave-like perspective. To great overhanging boul-
ders dripping, moss-grown, magnificent bunches

of maiden-hair clung; on mossy island-like rocks in the creek grew little groves of ferns and grasses and tiny trees. A glorious wealth of color below, a flaming lake in a vault of lapis lazuli above, a great wonderful silence, broken only by a solitary kingfisher swooping noisely down the creek, or the wind surging through the tree-tops like a suspended ocean.

Carmelita's gloom had vanished and she found herself wondering if only a few miles away lay a ranch whose gay spring gown was a bitter mockery. Her unquiet heart drowsed in a vague sweet languor. *Was* there a world beyond, or had a wall, higher than the highest peak, suddenly girdled the mountain and shut her in forever with her redwood lover? She looked at Tremaine and smiled at the fancy. He was balancing himself on a rock, angling desperately. His brows were frowning in the intensity of absorption and his nose was getting sunburnt. He caught his fish and glanced overhead.

" It is getting hot," he said. " Let us sit on the bank over yonder for a while."

She followed him to a green willow-garrisoned

patch of land beneath the bank, and he threw himself on the ground with a gratified sigh.

"It is deliciously cool here and this place is too lovely for fishing. I have never—never—seen any-thing so beautiful." He lay for a few moments, looking slowly about him, then turned to her. "You love it too," he said, "I have watched you. Whenever you raise your eyes you look as awed as if the gates of heaven had suddenly opened."

She held her arms up to the trees, then dropped them. "Yes," she said, "I love them."

"Do you come here often?"

"Yes. These trees are my friends like you have the mens. I have give them names, and, you no may believe, but they can talk."

"I do not doubt it." She was sitting on a fallen log a yard from him, but he felt as if she were in his arms. He felt *companioned* for the first time in his life. "I have lived for months alone in California forests and I have had a sense of inti-macy with trees that I never had for gabbling mortals. I doubt—I have doubted—if any human being could come as near." He pointed with his fishing rod to a madroña. "Look at that creature with her red kid gown and her bodice of burnished bronze. No woman is so slender and so well dressed as she. Once she was an Indian maiden, so perfect that Nature dared not let her die. That redwood there loved her as Romeo loved Juliet, and bitterness of race kept them apart until what we call death united them. When I die I pray I may become a redwood, for no destiny seems to me so eternal in its peace, so sublime in its strength."

Carmelita looked at him with dilating eyes and throbbing throat. The confession he moved her to had a different origin from the one that Geraldine had inspired.

"I will tell you"—she whispered.

"What?" he asked eagerly.

And then she told him her soul's romance. "When I see you yesterday," she said in conclusion, "I think my redwood have come down and walk on the ranch. Now I know why. You love the trees and know them like myself. No one else I ever know do that."

Tremaine sat up suddenly and took a package from the pocket of his basket. "Let us eat our luncheon," he said almost coldly. "It must be noon, and I am hungry."

They ate the rough sandwiches provided by the landlady of the Aguitas, and chatted of trifling things. At the meal's conclusion he produced his travelling cup, and she took it from him.

"I get you some water from the little fall," she said, "it is cold like mountain air in winter."

She waded into the creek and kneeling on a rock, caught the bubbles as they boiled over. Her long braids trailed on the stream and the water reflected her strong round limbs and perfect face. A mermaid was rising to the surface. Tremaine, who was on his feet, saw the reflection.

"Stay where you are for a moment," he said. "Do not move." He put his foot on a rock and swinging himself up the bank, tore a great bunch of maidenhair from its boulder. He leaped to the earth again, gathered an arm-full of ice grass and heavy ferns and waded out to Carmelita. She looked up at him inquiringly, but made no remonstrance as he twisted the maidenhair in her own bluish locks and thrust the ferns into the belt and neck of her gown.

"Now look at yourself," he said. "No gold-haired Lorlei was ever so wonderful as this," and together they leaned over the edge of the rock and looked down.

"I look si I grow out the ferns," she whispered, gazing at her luminous face beneath its waving crown. Then her head moved and she looked into Tremaine's reflected eyes. He was kneeling very close to her, for the rock was narrow. "Your eyes look like the sky when a storm coming and it turn from blue to gray"——she murmured, and then paused suddenly.

Nature, lying on her feathered couch in vast singing halls, opened her eyes, smiled, and dipping her white fingers in a fount beside her, sent upward a wave of golden ether, light as wine, sweet as the essences whereon the flowers supped. It surged over the two kneeling there, over and about them; it swept in a warm pungent current through their veins and mounted in flood tide to their heads. The outlines of the scene about them were gone, the world was a shimmering sea of light whose waves tossed perfume in the air, whose depths murmured the echo of all the bliss

the world had ever known. Then the wave receded, slowly, and in its wake was the chill of
death. Tremaine sprang to his feet, nearly over-
turning the stone, and Camelita, shivering from
head to foot, slipped into the water and waded to
the bank.

"My God!" thought Tremaine, "am I in love
with this girl? What damnable folly!" He strode
after her and caught up his fishing rod and basket. "Come! let us go home," he said, almost
roughly. "I have business this afternoon and
have stayed too long already."

V.

THE PRIEST AND THE WOMAN.

GERALDINE opened her door and stepped out into the court. The moon like a bashful school-girl looked at the earth over her curving arm. Clouds drifted before the budding stars, and in the far perspective of the picture seen through the open end of the court the shadows were thick as crowding ghosts. The trees were as quiet as if the hurrying wind had never quivered them, and not a sound broke that lonely stillness but the low continuous croaking of the frogs and the abrupt occasional hoot of the owl.

She shivered and drew her long cloak about her. " I wonder if any spot on earth is as quiet as this," she thought. " Sometimes I find myself believing that this ranch is really a wandering satellite, and that once it touched the earth and I stepped on." She left the court and wandered to the stile, and leaned against it for a few moments, then turned

it suddenly and walked down the hill to the road.
"It is horribly lonely," she thought, "but I must
have exercise, and the night is the only time. I
am mad with everlasting pacing up and down that
narrow gallery."

She walked on and on, starting at the shadows
and once screaming aloud as a soft bat brushed
her face, then forgetting fear and time in her own
unhappy thoughts. A hope was creeping on
stealthy hands and knees through her heart, born,
as many hopes are, of desire alone, but with vital
pulses. A dark mass loomed before her and she
knew that it must be the Mission. Then Hope
sprang to its feet, transformed to Will. Nevertheless the woman put her hands to her eyes with
a terrified cry and her body swayed as if the earth
were rolling beneath it. Then her limbs grew
rigid and she crept about the corner of the Mission and stood before the padre's house. One
bright window was like a jewel set in an iron wall,
and she advanced with careful steps and looked
through the thin cotton curtain. A man sat by
the chimney piece, his arms folded, his chin lowered on his chest, his hollowed eyes staring at the

empty fireplace. Geraldine sank inertly to the ground, her locked hands thrusting themselves unconsciously between the wide cracks in the adobe soil. "He is changed — changed" — she whispered with eyes turned to the past, then started in terror and wondered if she had screamed the words aloud.

But there was no sound in the house, and in a moment she raised herself, and turned as if to fly down the road, then went suddenly to the door and lifted the latch. The key had been turned. She knocked loudly on the thick oak panel. The padre came at once with a lamp in his hand.

"Who is it?" he asked kindly, for he was used to sudden calls.

He saw that a woman stood before him, but the fog ocean tossed before the moon. She made no answer. He held the lamp high above his head and it shone full on the white face and gleaming hair of the woman. With a hoarse cry, he fell back into the darkness, until she could see nothing but his blanched horrified face. She sprang forward, and taking the lamp from his relaxing fingers, grasped his arm and almost pushed him

13

into the study. He threw himself into a chair and covered his face with his trembling fingers, then suddenly sprang to his feet and pointed to the open door.

"Go!" he cried imperiously, "Go!"

"No, not yet," she said. "Let me stay a moment. I did not plan this visit, but now that I am here I must stay and speak." He turned from her and leaned his elbow on the chimney piece. "Do you know," she went on, hardly knowing what she said, "that I have lived here for more than a year? That I came here to be near you?"

He moved abruptly, but made no reply. "I shall stay near you until I die," she went on.

The priest's rigid fingers dug his face until the blood almost started. "O God, go!" he groaned, "Go! Go!"

She moved to approach him, but he turned swiftly and held out his arm.

"Do not come near me," he muttered.

Geraldine's cloak had slipped to the floor and her slender black-robed figure looked vibrant with suppressed emotion. Her heavy hair had tumbled from its pins, a flame had sprung from the clear fathomless depths of her perilous eyes. But as she held out her arms there was no voluptuous seduction in her manner. When a woman really loves and her heart is racked with agony and doubt, passion is frozen and art is forgotten. But a great cry escaped from her soul.

"Come! Come! Let us go where the church cannot follow us."

"Traitress!" he shouted, making no further attempt to control himself, "I hate you! How dare you come to me? What farce is this that brings you to bury yourself in an adobe hovel? Is it your idea of penance? You have come here to be near me and you will stay near me until you die! My God! what irony. Go! for I have nothing to say to you. Not a word."

She sprang forward with a low, frightened cry, but he retreated before her. "Not another word," he said, "I will not listen to it. Leave the house at once or I shall leave it."

For a moment the woman stood staring incredulously at him, but in his eyes was no relenting. Then with an imperious movement of her head, she sank slowly on her knees, raising her arm until the hand showed white against the dark.

"My father," she said, "I command you to hear my confession."

The priest caught his breath, and raised both clenched hands to his breast; but his faith was strong within him and he stood while she spoke.

VI.

IN THE SHADOW OF THE MISSION.

THE next evening Tremaine was walking among
the woods of the ranch, endeavoring to outstride
his own uneasy thoughts, when he was arrested
by a peculiar sound. A bird was calling and another was answering, but in the voice of the bird
who seemed to be on the ground, was a strangely
human note. He stood for some moments listening to the dialogue. The moon was flooding the
wood and he suddenly saw something move beneath a tree. It looked like a human form and
he put his hand mechanically to his pistol. At
the same moment he stepped on a crackling
branch, and in the face quickly turned to him he
recognized Carmelita.

She raised her finger warningly. "No make a
noise," she whispered, "but come si you like."

Tremaine, much mystified but nothing loath,

walked softly over to her, and sank on the ground
at her side.

"Listen." She raised her voice and warbled a
few strains, and Tremaine recognized the para-
doxical bird. A shower of notes fell from above
and for some moments the duo went on. Tremaine was deeply interested and felt that this
strange girl was about to reveal herself in a new
phase. He might be better off were he a thousand miles away from this ranch, but he felt a supreme content that he was not. Her small brown
hand lay on her knee and his own closed suddenly
over it. For a moment the duo was threatened,
and then Carmelita's voice went on in richer measure. After a time she paused and turned to him.

"You know what I do?" she asked.

"I do not."

"That poor bird—you no know how sad he is!
He losta his wife in the winter. The rain wash
her down from the nest one day. I find her and
bury her here by the tree. The poor bird he is so
lonely, señor! I come talk to him sometimes and
he feel better. To-night he tell me the whole
story again. You like to hear it, señor?"

Tremaine, who was divided between a desire to laugh and to kiss her, murmured that nothing would give him more pleasure.

" Well, you see it was like this. It rain so hard las winter that the nests no were strong in the trees. One day it no rain, but the clouds are black like the river, and this bird and his wife go to call on nother bird to see si they can borrow some grass to tie their nest more firm. But no one have any to spare; all are fraid like themselves. One bird ask them to stay in his house, but Enrique—that is the name de my bird—no want, for he and his wife no been marry long and they like be together. So, late they go home, and he kiss her and tell her no be fright, and tuck her in bed. Bime by she go to sleep, and he spread his wing over her, so she no get wet si the rain come; and bime by he go to sleep too. Then, señor, in the night come the rain. It is like the river jump to the sky and then fall down in one big sheet. It wash the nest from the tree, señor, and just sweep the poor little birds to the groun. Then it beat on them like stones, it come so fast. Enrique no could cry out and ask his wife how she is. He no can see, and bime by he no feel. . The rain beat his senses away. And the next morning, señor, when he wake, it have clear off, and there in the nest—he no was in himself—was poor little Manita, dead. The rain wash her life away. Oh, señor! he cry, cry, all the day. Then I come and find him with his wing over her, and his voice so sad I sit down in the mud and cry too. And then I dig the grave and the padre he make a little cross. And Enrique never leave this tree. I find him here always."

Tremaine bent his head and looked in her face. The story had touched him, but the girl's wild tender nature appealed to him more thrillingly than the sad little tragedy of the bird.

"And he never married again?" he asked, as comment was required.

Carmelita's eyes flashed. "Of course not! He no love her ?"

Tremaine stood up suddenly. "I have a fancy to see the old Mission by moonlight," he said. "Will you come with me? or—would you rather go home. It is late."

"I go to the Mission," said Carmelita obligingly.

She rose to her feet and warbled a few notes. A plaintive voice responded, and she followed Tremaine down the path.

"He say good-night. You hear? He is very sorry I go."

"Undoubtedly." He made no further attempt at conversation until they reached the Mission, when again his conscience smote him and he asked her if she should not be at home.

"Are you sure your aunt will not be worried? It must be nearly eleven o'clock."

"My aunt have the other childrens and always I do what I feel like. Sometimes when I go to the mountain and no feel like come home I sleep in a tree that been eat out by the fire and my aunt she no mind. She love me, but you see she have so many others," and she pushed a box against the wall and sat down.

The supreme isolation of her life, conveyed in the careless almost absent words, again gave Tremaine a sense of having touched her soul with his. His own loneliness was so appalling! And now, a piece of driftwood on the stream of Circumstance, he had floated to an island of security and

peace, bliss and communion, with Nature to mur-
mur banns and blessings—and he must touch and
drift on! As yet no desire had entered into his
love. He had outgrown the indiscriminate and
omnipresent sensuality of youth, and beautiful
and half clothed as the girl was, her kinship to
Nature was too close for him to regard her by the
standard of other women; her kinship with him
so absolute that passion could be but the demand
for closer spiritual union—when Nature commanded her subtlest interpretations. The feeling
he had for her now was one of great and perfect
friendship. She had stolen into his nature com-
pleting and quickening. She had put her ten
fingers in rapid succession upon every note of his
being and drawn fullest measure of sound from
each. The world sang to him once more.

Carmelita sat motionless, her head on her hand.
She had made no attempt to define what she had
felt in the creek yesterday. Something had come,
and she held it close and hid its face.

"Talk to me," he said. "Tell me something about
yourself. Who were your father and mother?"

"My father was Joaquin Murietta." Carme-

lita's pride in her erratic parent had not declined
with ethical advancement; her life had been too
solitary, her nature was too romantic.

"No? I had no idea you were of such distinguished birth. And your mother?"

She told him that fair mother's history, and he
listened with great interest. "That is romantic!"
he exclaimed when she had finished. "I knew
you did not come from the vegetable garden.
And you—you with such parentage, you are out
of place in this commonplace existence. Who
will you marry, I wonder." He uttered the words
idly. He did not picture her the wife of any man.

Carmelita parted her lips. The air seemed to
have left her lungs. "I never marry," she said
coldly, after a moment, but the knuckles of her
hand bruised her cheek. "Alway I live like
this. The padre say so, and I know."

Tremaine set his teeth suddenly, and she rose
and leaned against the pillar by her box. He
gazed at her for a moment and then paid her a
compliment with angry vehemence.

"How beautiful you are!" he said. "I cannot
help telling you that. Do you know that in the

world I come from I have never seen a woman so perfect as you?"

She turned to him and smiled, the warm blood rushing to her face and throat. Then, with a sudden impulse of coquetry, the first of her life, she swept her hair from its braids and shook the silky web about her. It clung to her like inky mist, and through it peered her startled face with its parted lips and appealing eyes. The action was exquisite, the first tribute of a woman to the man who had stirred her heart from the calm of its birth, and Tremaine's pulses leaped and fought against their prisoning walls. He sprang to his feet and his eyes flashed their answer to the appeal of hers. Oh! but the hour and the woman were witching. The night pulsed about them! The very air was drugged with the perfume of the spring flowers, the heavy scent of locust blossoms.

He folded his arms and set his shoulders against the pillar behind him.

"Your hair is very beautiful," he said coldly. "Were I an artist I should paint you so." And he stood regarding her calmly from beneath his eyes' concealing lids. He needed no brush to com-

memorate the scene: the great silent expanse,
rolling away like a sea of reflected silver until it
met and broke against the far-off mountains; the
ruinous old Mission, grand in its simple resigna-
tion to poverty and neglect; the beautiful woman,
with her eager passionate face and wonderful
glory of hair; it was etched into his brain.

She turned from him and began braiding her
hair, her flesh chilled, as if the night wind were
the breath of mid-winter. As she thrust the
strands back and forth with awkward fingers her
downcast eyes caught sudden view of her bare
legs. Blushing a hot painful red she shrank back
into the shadow of the pillar, yet feeling that
there was no night which would cover her naked-
ness from this man's gaze. Her pulse throbbed
against her swelling throat and she trembled from
head to foot with shame. What must he think
of her? The women he knew did not dress like
that. Why, why, had she not thought of this before? And for a moment a demon within her
raved and bit and cursed the fate which had
wrought her ignorance.

Her instinct was to fly into the Mission and

bolt herself in a cell until he should have gone;
but pride, blind but peremptory, forbade her to
provoke misinterpretation. She bit her lips and
in a moment the muscles of her throat relaxed.

"Buenas noches," she said, shaking her hair
about her. "No come with me. I go to see the
señora," and she walked down the road with head
erect and burning face. Tremaine did not follow.
He was puzzled, but glad to be alone.

She went straight to Lindavista, but when she
reached Geraldine's door it was some time before
it was opened. Then Carmelita gave a little cry
of horror, forgetting her own trouble.

"Geraldinita!" she cried, "what is the matter?
You are ill, no? You are white like the virgin in
the Mission."

"Come in," said Geraldine, grasping her hand
eagerly. "I am so glad you are here. Stay with
me to-night."

"Si, I stay. But why you are so pale?"

"I wish to God I were paler," exclaimed the
woman passionately. She pushed the girl into a
chair, sitting by her. "What brought you? Is
there any more trouble?"

"Geraldina, I go to ask you to give me something, and you no will mind, no? for I never ask for nothing before."

"Ask for what you want, my dear girl. You are welcome to all I have."

"I no want much. Only one old skirt—*long*—that you no wear any more."

"But my child, what will you do with a train?"

"I no want a train, only a dress to cover my legs—all roun'!"

Geraldine was too wise to ask questions, and she went into the next room, returning in a moment with a black skirt.

"Take this," she said. "I am very glad to get rid of it. It never suited me."

"But it is too good, Geraldina. You no have nothing more old?"

"I shall never wear this again and it is two years old at least. Here, put it on." She threw it over the girl's head and fastened the belt.

Carmelita walked down the room, surveying herself over each shoulder and down the front. Her self-respect was restored, and she felt dignified and worthy to be the daughter of her mother.

"They no can see my legs now," she exclaimed triumphantly. "I no look *indecente* any more."

"You never looked indecent," said Geraldine indignantly. "Who has said such a thing to you?"

"No one say to me——" and then she threw her arms about Geraldine and broke into wild, convulsive weeping. Geraldine drew her down on to the divan, and putting her head on the girl's shoulder, wept also. Her grief was less violent but it was more hopeless, for youth with its ignorance of life was behind her.

"I no know si I am happy or sorry," sobbed Carmelita.

But the woman had no such doubt.

VII.

ALEXANDER TREMAINE.

"I HAD almost forgotten," said Geraldine the next morning. "I have twenty dollars for you."

"What!"

"It came yesterday. It is a greenback, but you must have gold or you would never realize its value." And she threw back the heavy stuffs of the divan and took from a drawer a heavy piece of gold, new and bright.

The girl was unfeignedly delighted. "I go to the Aguitas to-day," she cried, "and buy some closes for the children and plenty beans and flour. Geraldina, I love you."

Geraldine put her arm about the girl's shoulders. "You have not yet told me your trouble," she said. "Some day perhaps you will. Remember that I am your friend and that I love you."

Carmelita turned away her head to hide the blood that had jumped to her face. "I no know, Geraldina. I no think I ever tell."

14

"What can it be?" thought Geraldine.

That afternoon Carmelita went with her gold to
the Aguitas. This landmark of civilization was
a good four miles from her home, but she walked
the distance swiftly and reached the place before
dark. The porch in front of the "hotel" was
crowded with excited groups discussing the coming of the sheriffs on the morrow; but even the
young men were too absorbed to notice her, and
she slipped into the store and made her purchases.
It was a question of deep moment, the spending
of those twenty dollars, and when it was finally
settled, and the man had been instructed to give
the heavier things to Espinoza when he should
call, the porch was deserted and night had come.

She put her bundle under her arm and was
about to strike across the road, thankful that she
would go unseen, when she heard the sound of
voices in a large room adjoining the store. Even
this fragment of the world appealed to her curiosity at times and after a moment's hesitation she
stepped to the window and peered within. For
many moments she stood motionless, too fascinated to move.

The large room was bare and uncarpeted, but huge logs crackled hospitality in the open fire-place, reddening the ugly peeling walls with their leaping glare. In the centre of the room, gathered close about a table, were four men, bearded, dark, desperate looking, their sombreros pulled low over watchful eyes, their hands filled with shuffling cards, small heaps of gold glittering beside them. Silent, calm as sphinxes, they saw their piles augment or disappear, while the men who to-morrow might be without a roof to their heads, crowded about with greedy gaze and muttered wagers. In a corner a man was making a captured bat smoke a cigarette, and by the hearth crouched the old Indian holding his ghoulish hands to the flames.

"Come," said a voice behind Carmelita's shoulder. "Do not look any more. There may be a fight any moment."

Carmelita started, almost dropping her bundle, but Tremaine took it from her. "I will go home with you," he said. "It is too late for you to be on this part of the ranch alone."

They walked for some distance in silence. The

moon was not up yet and the road had little light, but Carmelita felt as if the ground had turned buoyant as air, and vague disturbance fled.

"I have no right to this," thought Tremaine, "but it is for the last time." " Why have you put on that long dress ?" he demanded abruptly. " I like the short one much better. It suits you, and that long shapeless thing does not."

" I like," said Carmelita briefly. "And it is very strange si you no like, for you no can be use to the short skirt where you live before."

" I like what I am not used to. You were not afraid to take this walk alone?" he added quickly.

" I no think; I want so much to get the things; but I am glad you come."

" What things?"

" I find an old certificate, and the señora send to the city and sell for me. She give to me las night one big gold piece, and I go to the Aguitas to buy the closes for the childrens, and many other things that no would interest you, señor."

"And what did you get for yourself?"

" Nothing, for I no want. The señora she give to me this dress."

"When?" asked Tremaine quickly.

She hesitated. "Las night."

A flash of inspiration came to Tremaine and for a moment he saw the objects about him less distinctly. "She loves me!" he thought exultingly, and he repeated the words many times. He put out his arms with a swift motion. There was an ache in the muscles and he held them so rigidly that they were cramped. Then he dropped them suddenly. She was a little ahead and saw nothing. If she had she would have sprung to him as naturally as a forest queen springs to its mate.

"Talk to me," he said. "Say something. I like to hear your fancies. Tell me about your birds and flowers."

"I tell you one thing I have think for a long time, ever since the señora tell me the history," she answered, willing to please him, and finding the subject a congenial one. "You have hear of Semiramis, no? She was a great queen before— Babylon I think."

"Yes, I have heard."

"You remember she have the hanging gardens on her palace, no? Well, this is what I think.

Nature she have the palace in the earth—the flowers they describe to me, and the house of Semiramis no can compare. You no may believe, but I do, and I believe it is right under us, and California is the hanging garden de her."

" I shouldn't wonder! "

"And sometimes in the night when it is warm and the air so sweet I no can bear to sleep inside, I see *her*. She is tall like the big oaks, but she shine like a star through the fine mist—and she sweep her train over her hills, and the wild flowers kiss her feet and the air whisper with a sound I never hear any other time cept when I kneel and hold my ear one foot from the groun. You ever hear that sound, señor? It no is roar, or buzz, or hum, but all three and low. I often listen, for when you stand high you no hear."

" I have heard it when I have been lying alone in the woods on a summer's day. But go on. What are those frogs talking about?"

" Listen! you no can tell? I know. They sing the funeral mass for the dead birds."

" Never mind any more," said Tremaine harshly, " there is your home." He threw the bundle to the ground. "Give me your hands," he said, "I have something to say to you."

She looked at him wonderingly and then gave him both warm quivering hands. He crushed them roughly against his breast and brought his flushed face close to her paling one. His self-control was leaving him and his knees shook suddenly. The words came with difficulty, but he said them.

"Carmelita! I am Alexander Tremaine."

And he dropped her hands and went down the road, and out of her sight.

VIII.

AT THE FOOT OF THE CROSS.

THE padre was sitting by his table, his face buried in his hands, when he heard the outer door open and a woman's footsteps rushing toward his study. He sprang to his feet, the cold drops starting on his forehead, then sank back with a quick sigh of relief. It was Carmelita.

He looked at her for a moment, unseeingly, then rose suddenly and put out his hand.

"My child, what is it?" he asked. "What has happened to you?"

She pressed her hands about her throat as if she would speak, then threw herself headlong to the floor and lay on her face at his feet. She made no sound, but she shook like a wounded panther that has crawled to a familiar spot to die.

The padre sat down and folded his arms. He knew that the time had not come to speak. He divined the cause of her agony. The day he had

turned his eyes to the organ platform and seen
the commanding head of the stranger he had felt
a prophetic sense of its coming, and since, he had
passed them twice. He had intended to seek
Tremaine and ask him to go before any harm
should be done. And now it was too late. While
man hesitates love flies with lightning in his
wings, and strikes.

Once, as he sat watching her mortal woe, a
question almost unconsciously drifted through his
mind. Which would be worse: to marry an ignorant Mexican and spend her life in a dirty hovel
with a swarm of half-naked children and not a
memory of youth, or to have known the splendid
agony of love and loss and despair? He thrust
the question aside with a shudder. He knew the
bitterness of memories.

The girl's quivering body grew quiet and she
lay motionless for a few moments, then rose to
her feet and stood looking down on him with
sullen demand.

He rose also. "Do not speak," he said, "I
know—I know."

He walked rapidly up and down the room, striving to think of some comfort to give her; but he knew the futility of words to heal such wounds. Suddenly his eyes fell on a black curtain which hung before a recess in the wall, and with a rapid stride he stood before it. He turned his eyes to hers for one expressive second, then flung the curtain aside and Carmelita made the quick involuntary sign of the cross. In the recess was an altar with crucifix and lighted candles. The priest raised his eyes and his hand, pointing upward, then, his eyes meeting hers again, he lowered his arm slowly and pointed to the steps of the altar. Carmelita crossed the room and fell on her knees, pressing her arms about the altar. Then the priest went out and left her alone.

IX.

THREE CITIZENS OF CERRITOS.

"WE'VE got two pistols apiece, sir," said the sheriff. " I hope you're fixed."

" Yes," said Tremaine. " But I don't wish any dispossessing done to-day. We will talk to the men and see if they have any suggestions to make. Hawkins will explain."

He sprang on his horse, the sheriffs and Hawkins got into the wagon, and they went down the road that led through the ranch. The sheriff and deputies had arrived at twelve o'clock the night before, and no plans had been made.

" It's a stroke of luck you come when you did," said Hawkins, " the squatters was just beginnin' to ketch on to the fact that Mr. Tremaine was himself. I persuaded him to go by the genteel name of Smith fur a while, fur he would ride all over the ranch, and if they had knowed who he was his life wouldn't have been worth a damn."

The sheriff eyed Tremaine. " He's good'n big,

and he don't look like he'd take water too easy. Guess they wouldn't enjoy a tussle with him. Hanged if I would. But he looks like he knowed it was a serious business."

"Yes, he looks a deal more serious than when he come. I guess he's looked into things a bit, but he's a man as don't say much." He raised his voice. "Castro's house is on the other side of the hill, sir," he called to Tremaine. "Better have yer pistol ready. He's the wust o' the lot."

Tremaine broke from his thoughts with a start of relief and spurred his horse to the top of the hill. A neat farm, fenced with branches, lay below. Smoke was curling from the chimney and an old woman sat in the door way. The scene was peaceful, and signs of moving there were none. The birds twittering in the trees seemed no more confidently established in their nests. Castro's parents were too old to reason. He told them they were to stay, and they gave no thought to exile.

"Well, of all the gall!" exclaimed the sheriff. "But that's just like Castro."

They drove through the gate and the old woman pushed her ragged white hair out of her eyes and grinned a yellow and solitary tooth into view, while with one skinny hand she scratched her mahogany cheek. A facetious traveller, seeing her once at the Aguitas, had christened her Cleopatra and the name had clung to her ever since. Not that the squatters had ever heard of the dark and limber queen, but they knew that a joke was intended and were ready to keep it up. The sheriff, with his hand on his hip pocket, jumped from the wagon and went up to the old woman, followed by the others. Tremaine rode to the porch, but did not dismount.

"Can we see yer son?" asked the sheriff.

Cleopatra mumbled something and pointed over her shoulder. But she had no need to call her son. He was not attending to his vaquero duties during this momentous crisis, and as he heard the sheriff's voice he gave a hoarse growl and strode to the door like an angry lion from its lair. As he saw Tremaine his jaws began to work and his huge nostrils dilated. But Tremaine gave him a long gaze from beneath his drooping lids and in a moment he turned uneasily to the others and blusteringly demanded what they wanted.

"We want to talk to you a bit."

"I no got nothing to say."

"But we have to you," said the sheriff. He rolled a quid to the other side of his mouth and seating himself on the window sill swung his leg as an accompaniment to his words.

"Now look here, Castro, I know you and you know me. What I've got to say you kin jest believe, you bet. If you want to stay on this place you've got to pay rent or buy. The place ain't yourn. It's Mister Tremaine's. The law has give it to him—square, square, and no joke; and you've either got to pay or git."

"The law be damned," yelled Castro, "I no leaving this place si you bring the army with you. I die by the door first. The place no is Señor Tremaine's. I have before and it is mine."

"That'll do, Castro. Just tone down that voice of yourn, will yer? We're none of us deef. Now, if you've made up your mind not to rent or buy, Mr. Hawkins tells me that the Sennor Tremaine has made up his mind to give yer the price o' yer crops; and in common decency you ought to treat him as well's he treats you and not give him no more trouble."

" Señor Dios! " shouted Castro, " I lika choke his dirty gold down his throat. I no want his moneys. I want *my* land. Now go to hell." And he strode into the house, gnashing his teeth, muttering and growling.

" Well," said the sheriff, sliding from the window seat and stamping his foot into his boot. There's only fight with him, that's certain. We'll try somewheres else. Looks as if there was goin' to be reel gay times."

They drove down the road, one of the deputies throwing his legs over the back of the seat and absently toying with his pistol, and in a short time they drew up before another hacienda. Here, neatness did not prevail and the crop was uneven and straggling, as if the hand that had guided the plough had felt little nerve for its work. Four or five ragged children were playing on the porch, and at the sound of the wheels a large Mexican woman waddled to the door. She wore a solitary garment of calico, and acres of fat quivered serenely upon other acres, as she walked.

"Scott! What a fairy," observed the sheriff. "But she won't cuss, that's one comfort. She couldn't get up the steam."

The woman made no courtesy as the men approached her. She looked sullen and indifferent. "Buenas dias! sennora," said the sheriff heartily. "Can we see yer husband?"

"He feeda the pigs," said the woman. "José, go calla him," and she turned her back and returned to the stove.

One of the youngsters disappeared around the corner of the house, and in a moment returned with a tall man dressed in overalls and a flannel shirt. His mouth was set under his heavy beard, as if apprehension threatened to master him. He gave his head a little jerk, then stood waiting for the men to speak.

"My good man," said the sheriff, "before lettin' the law take its course, Mister Tremaine wants to know if yer have any propositions to make. If yer want to rent, the terms won't be very hard, and if yer want to buy, yer can do it on the instalment plan."

The man folded his arms. "I no got one cents,"

he said. "I got two pigs. When I killing them, si I no can sell my horse, the childrens starve. I no can do it nothing more."

"Well, you *be* in a bad way," assented the sheriff. "But the sennor will buy yer crops."

The man laughed. "Looka them," he said. "How much they worth? Much better we starve and have done."

"Then you have no plans to sergest?" said the sheriff, rising from the box on which he had sociably seated himself.

"How the poor man can maka the plan? The rich man do it that and the poor man eata the grass."

"Then yer're ready to go without trouble?"

The man looked at his children and the blood blazed to his face.

"Oh! whatte I can do?" he cried. "Si you putting me out I mus go! It no is use to fight. I telling them that. The law taking from us our own and we no can do it nothing. Take it! Putting out the wife and childrens but I no can stay to see," and he fled around the angle of his house.

"Come," said Tremaine hurriedly. "Let us go."

15

"I hope he's not goin' to be soft about it," said the sheriff to Hawkins as they rode off, "because he'd do no good if he was. They're a lazy lot, anyhow. They hav'n't got a cent left, that's certain, but they might jest as well starve on the high-road and let him have his land. What a daisy place he could make of it!"

The next farm in their progress belonged to a "white squatter." The children swarming over the porch this time were white-haired, but so sunburnt that they were few shades fairer than their Mexican brothers. A woman was sitting in the door mending a child's dress, and her husband was digging in the field. He stood up and watched the approaching visitors with a scowl. He had been a good-natured man, but the hardships and worry of the last year had turned his blood to acid. As the men alighted and spoke to his wife he walked forward and stood before them.

"What d'yer want?" he demanded savagely, for he suspected their errand.

The man of law said, with a friendly smile, "I'm only the sheriff—don't go and get skeered, though," he added, as the man paled under his weather-beaten skin. "We're willin' to make terms if you've got anything ter sergest."

"I ain't got nothin' ter suggest," growled the man, "and I ain't goin' ter leave." But his pitiable attempt at bravado did not deceive even his wife, and she put the rag she was mending to her eyes and began to cry silently.

"But I'm afraid yer'll have ter," said the sheriff, putting his hands into his pockets and regarding the wretched man with a bland smile. "Law is law, yer know, and if yer don't pay or go, we'll be under the painful necessity of puttin' y'out 'bout this time to-morrow. I'm sorry, but them's my orders, and I'm only a servant of the law."

"Come to-morrow," said the man with inadvertant significance.

"Aha!" thought the sheriff. "Something's in the wind." But he made no comment. "Do you all feel alike on this question—that yer won't budge till yer're fired?"

"Yes," said the man sullenly, "that's the way we feel. The land's ourn, not that thief Tremaine's. Oh, that's him, is it. Well, let him be damned. I fur one am willin' he should hear my opinion of 'im. If he takes the land what's mine in spite of the law, he's a thief, nothin' mor'n less. You kin arrest me if yer like. Nothin' could be wuss than 'tis now."

"Oh, we won't arrest yer; for bein' wusted, it's natral you should feed a little riled, and words don't do no harm. It's only when shots is fired that yer run risks. Sometimes bullets hit too hard and then yer're strung up. But yer're too hard on Mister Tremaine. He intends to give yer the price o' yer crops."

Tremaine writhed on his saddle for the third time that day. Every time the sheriff made that offer he felt as mean and paltry as if a starving woman had begged of him in the street and he had thrown her a nickel.

The man laughed aloud. "He'd better keep it," he said with a sneer. "He might want it to buy one of them silk shirts with, he's got on. We don't need it. The lawyer didn't want no money fur what he didn't do!"

Tremaine spurred his horse and galloped down the road, the men hurrying after him.

"He's a fool, that man," exclaimed the sheriff, as he lashed his horse. "He ain't got no right to be one minute alone on this ranch. They'd as soon kill 'im as look at 'im."

X.

A BROKEN MEDITATION.

LATE that night Tremaine was walking slowly up and down before the Aguitas revolving a problem that had temporarily driven even Carmelita from his mind. What should he do in regard to these squatters? If he turned them out to starve on the highway he would feel no better than any common murderer who cut a man's throat for the sake of his pocket book. The law was on his side, but he was almost glad that at last he felt it a duty to set some law at defiance. And yet he was not prepared to hand over his land bodily to these men. He was a generous man, but his business faculty had been carefully trained by a close and long-headed New England father. And would he do them any material good? That was another question. An unfortunate experience had made him sceptical. He regarded Henry George as the most enlightened of political economists, but even his theories would be apt to warp if the application was too premature. In ultimate equality he had not a grain of belief: so long as human nature retained its primitive ingredients, the clever or the lucky man would always get to the top. Nor was it desirable. In that heaven of the famished socialist, with its stunting perfection and chloroforming monotony, no man with brains or passion would wish to exist. It read well, but the application would be deadly. For the small and easy ambitions that were left, no man would care to compete, and the most pungent quality of life—variety—would be gone. Nevertheless he had it in his mind to give these squatters their farms if only by way of experiment. It would be interesting to watch the outcome. He was inclined to provide for the unfortunates in some way, and perhaps to give them their farms was the easiest solution of the matter.

He felt a strange sensation—as if an eagle had rushed by him, tearing his hair as she passed; and then he knew that a bullet had gone through his hat. He stepped back onto the porch of the Aguitas, and standing behind a pillar, cocked his pistol. The moon was up and the night was still. For a half-hour he waited for the man to betray himself, but the half-hour passed and there was no sound but the music of the frogs.

" It's that fiend, Castro," he thought. " I should enjoy getting a shot at him."

Another half-hour passed and then he stepped into his room and closed the door. " Whoever it is I'll hear from him again," he thought. "And it's time to go to bed; I must be up early to-mor-row." He moved about the room, feeling for a candle, then stopped short and listened. There was a crackling of paper under his door, followed by a sound of running feet. Before he could reach the porch a man was galloping down the road. He fired a shot after the burly figure, but a loud laugh was the only answer, and he opened the missive directed to him and read it by the moon's vivid light. From an almost unintelligi-ble jargon of Spanish and English he gathered that if he did not take the stage the next morning he would swing from the highest tree on the Cer-ritos ranch before night. The rest of the page

was given over to a choice assortment of vitupera-
tive epithets, and was signed with the names of
sixty squatters.   Tremaine flung the note into the
dust of the road and returned to the house.

XI.

IN VASQUEZ' CAÑON.

THE next morning when Tremaine spoke of his adventure, the sheriff begged him to return to San Francisco. "They'll kill yer sure's fate," he said, "and you can't do no good by stayin'. We kin do the business better without yer."

"I shall not go," said Tremaine. "Do you suppose I am going to let the brutes run me off the ranch? Besides the satisfaction I shall have in seeing the thing through, I have private reasons for wishing to remain until the squatters are actually dispossessed."

"Well, you can't say I havn't warned yer. But I'll betcher twenty dollars to two bits I ship a corpse back to Frisco."

Tremaine laughed and rode out of the Aguitas yard. As he turned the corner of the building he came face to face with Espinoza, who had evidently been lying in wait for him. The man

glanced hurriedly around, then slipped a note into
Tremaine's hand." "From Carmelita," he said
nervously. "No say nothing for the love of
heaven, señor."

"No; have no fear; I will not betray you. And
I may as well tell you now, you are to keep your
land—your hacienda."

Before the bewildered man could reply, Tremaine had spurred his horse and was galloping
down the road. He did not draw rein until he
reached a wood near the Mission. Then he tore
open the note with the impatience born of delay.

"Oh, señor, go! go!" it ran. "They kill you si
you stay. Castro he swear and las night they
have the meeting and they all are very mad and
say they shoot you si you come near the housses.
And I—I—señor, I mus tell you si you hate me.
Before you come I jump on the table in Castro's
field one night and I do it all I can to make them
hate you; I make them wild by what I say and I
beg them to *kill* you, señor, and they go crasy
when I speke and shout they will. And now they
go to do it and it is my faul! Castro say he and

plenty mens write and tell you si you no go they hang you to the tree. They want to fright you so you go with the sheriffs and no make them shoot and be hang up. I know you no go for them, but I ask you go, señor. I write this on my knees and I beg you go and no be kill. And I think si I ask that one thing you do it.

"CARMELITA."

Tremaine quickly folded the brown paper missive as the sheriffs came rattling down the road. He could not grant her prayer, but he wished that a continent was between them.

The hacienda they had planned to attack first belonged to a Mexican named Lopez, and they had sent him warning the night before. As Tremaine, who was riding some distance ahead of the wagon in spite of the warning calls of the sheriff, emerged from the grove of trees before the man's farm, he saw some fifty or sixty men standing in a row before the door. As he approached them each raised his gun to his shoulder and put his finger to the trigger. Tremaine set his teeth, but the danger gave him the first sense of stimulation he had felt that morning. He was not excited, but he was in a mood to sullenly pit with fate itself and ask no quarter. He raised the bridle of his mustang and dashing down the path, sprang to the ground and had flung a man aside and entered the house before the squatters realized whether he was a man or an apparition. He seized a chair and threw it out of the window, and then the whole body of them surged into the room and surrounded him with furious curses and brandishing fists. He paid no attention, but flung a mattress after the bed, and at the same moment the wagon drove up.

"God!" cried the sheriff. "The man's clean mad," and leaping from the wagon he rushed into the house, fingering his revolver and followed by the others. The squatters, poor wretches, were intimidated by the determination and contempt of Tremaine and his men, and stood back like whipped curs. The sheriff saw his advantage.

"Now look yere," he said, throwing a sack of beans into the open, then turning to the men with his knuckles on his hips. "You see we ain't afraid, don't yer, and yer can't do nothin'? If yer kill us there is plenty more where we come from, and rope enough to swing the whole damned lot o' yer. If yer kill Mr. Tremaine he's got a wife who'll fight for the property after 'im. He's got money and law behind 'im and you ain't got nothin'. So jest clear out and we'll do what we come for. What's more, the first man as raises his gun drops. Now git."

The men sullenly withdrew, and one of the deputies was told to watch them while the others carried out the household goods and laid them on the ground. The men, thoroughly cowed, made no further attempt to resist, and when the work was done Tremaine and his men departed unmolested. They dispossessed two other families, with no disturbance beyond the crying and maledictions of the women, and then Tremaine announced his intention of leaving his comrades to finish the work by themselves.

"There will be no further trouble," he said, "and I'm sick of the business."

"Well, I'm doggoned!" exclaimed the sheriff. "You don't mean to tell me that yer goin' to meander around this ranch by yerself? If they git a chance at yer with no one to tell the tale they'll riddle yer, sure pop."

"They'll do no more to-day," said Tremaine.

His tone silenced dispute, and the sheriff shrugged his shoulders and drove away.

Tremaine rode along listlessly, giving his horse the bridle. The road lay by the river, already sinking and half choked by the trees and shrubs washed down by winter storms. But the poppies were red on the banks, and the yellow lupins mocked the corruption below. The sun like a golden nautilus skimmed the concave deep. The birds sang in the trees as if the world had stopped to listen and knew naught of sorrow nor care. Only a hare, sitting by an oak-tuft, suddenly raised his long ears at sight of man, then fled wildly into the distance.

It is a pretty trick of authors to make nature ever in sympathy with man, but as a matter of fact she seldom is. Where one person, stunned with grief, hears the wind moan in sympathy, and watches a leaden sky drop heavy tears, unnumbered gaze with straining eyes across a radiant landscape and wonder, in the egoism of their grief,

how the men can work in the fields as they did
yesterday, how the birds can sing, the warm breeze
scatter the perfume of the flowers abroad, how
the very earth does not cease to revolve. As for
another phase of the matter, Shakespeare, that
master of tricks, yet makes Richard III. on the
morning of the battle of Bosworth most perti-
nently say:

" The sun will not be seen to-day:
The sky doth frown and lour upon our army.
Not shine to-day! Why, what is that to me
More than to Richmond? for the self-same heaven
That frowns on me, looks sadly upon him."

Tremaine, usually at one with nature in any
mood, was depressed by her to-day. Carmelita
was nature's favorite child and the mother suggested the daughter. Moreover he was not on
good terms with himself. He had sacrificed his
better promptings to that determination to win at
cost of man or right which is in the blood of every
Californian of this generation: the legacy inherited from the men whose fever for gold and hardships in an unbroken country had made the individual paramount to the race. "I suppose it is
the brute in me," he thought. " We Californians

LOS CERRITOS. 241

are made of nature's raw material, character, in-
tellect, genius, all, and are half barbarians in consequence. I feel savage yet and hot for a fight."

The road turned and passed the head of a gulch.
The place was unusually lonely even for a thinly-
settled country, and lying between two high and
thickly wooded hills was sombre on that brilliant
day. Long strands of sickly green moss, like
witches' unkempt beards, draped every limb, and
no flowers grew among the rocks. Half way down
the cañon was a rude hut, and above it grew heavy
willows, casting their long shadows over a deserted dwelling that no man passed at night alone.

"It is the hut of Vasquez," thought Tremaine,
"and will be worth having seen."

He rode down the gulch, his horse stumbling
over the loose stones. The bandit had not been
grasping in the matter of land, for he could not
have raised a crop there.

When Tremaine reached the hut he dismounted
and went within. There were only two rooms and
no furniture except a rusty old stove and a bench.
Miserable as the articles were they would have
been appropriated long ago in this land of poverty,

16

had there been a man in the neighborhood who dared go to the ruined home of the outlaw and brave his ghost. More than one, galloping by the gulch at night, swore that he had seen a shadowy form flying up and down as if pursued by the demons who were doubtless his present associates.

Tremaine sat down on the bench in the kitchen and lit a cigar. He liked the quiet of the place and it did not mock him with memories of Carmelita. This gloomy cañon did not suit her. Nature had wrought her in spring when the blood was red and warm in her own veins, imagination rich with the awakened instinct of creation. She should lie forever in banks of wild-flowers, or splash through a wondrous creek gorgeous with primitive color and a pink mist creeping over the mountain above—

He rose impatiently and went out to the open. The tethered mustang, already fond of him, raised his nose from the grass, coaxing for a longer meal. But Tremaine was in no mood to linger. He was about to untie the lariat when something hard hit his shoulder and glided over his arm.

The low infuriated cry of a woman, a howl of

pain and baffled purpose, and in a fateful instant
two men had rushed together and grappled. In
the thick side of Castro's buckskin jacket was the
knife Carmelita had plunged there as he flung
the lasso, and this Tremaine strove to wrench out,
for neither man had time to draw his pistol. But
in that first sudden confusion he saw nothing but
the face of Carmelita. It was transfigured. Not
a trace of its tenderness remained. The teeth
were clenched with fierce cruelty behind tense
bloodless lips, the eyes were blazing with lust of
blood, the whole face as terrible in its ferocity as
that of a tigress wrenched of her young.

"Kill him! Kill him!" she screamed. "He go
to rope you and drag you like the dog. O Dios!
si I no come after him!"

Then Tremaine lost consciousness of everything
but the blind instinct to kill. All the pent-up
passion of years, stirred, but repressed of late,
leaped through his veins and boiled in his head.
In that moment he was as great a brute as the
one he fought. The men grappled like bears in a
death embrace, each snatching at the other's pistol
and wrenching to right and left as fingers and hip-

pockets approached too near. If Tremaine had
only a Derringer! If he could only tear the veins
from the man's body and get him prone that he
might stamp him to jelly. Again he made a pass
for the low swinging knife—his own was flattened
between two hot, straining bodies—and again,
Castro, roaring like a bull, and making furious
lunges with his jaws, tightened his embrace, until
Tremaine felt as if ribs and lungs were being
ground to paste. But if Castro had muscles of
iron, Tremaine's were those of steel.

The two men's faces were close together, black,
murderous. Their savage breath mingled. Suddenly Castro flung the whole weight of his huge
body on Tremaine's left forearm and the wrist
bone cracked like a china plate. A knife flashed
in the air and through the thin silk shirt into
Tremaine's left shoulder. Then with a mad shout
of triumph Castro flung the wounded man to the
ground and swung his right hand for his pistol.
But Carmelita had it. She had not wept nor
prayed. She had watched her chance. As Castro
stabbed Tremaine she plucked the pistol from its

sheath on his hip, and he turned to find it pointed at him. She could not miss that broad target.

"Go," she whispered hoarsely; but her hand was steady. "Go, Castro, or I shoot. Touch him and I kill you dead."

Castro, with purple, shaking lips, glared from her to Tremaine. His antagonist's face was white and the eyes were closed. Was he dead already? The lasso lay near him and seemed to twist itself into a hangman's rope. Castro ran down the gulch as if the law was already at his heels, and Carmelita knew that he would not return.

XII.

A GHOST.

THE pistol dropped from Carmelita's hand, the ferocity ebbed from her face, her womanhood surged to the surface once more.

"Dios de mi alma!" she sobbed, "he is dead."

She fell on her knees and bent over him. "Si he is dead he is mine," she thought, and exultation kept pain at bay for a moment. "It no can be wrong to kiss him now si he is dead," and she laid her cheek to his, then put both hands about his face and kissed him on the mouth. She drew his head up to her warm, round bosom and laid it there unheeding the weight of his body.

"I stay here till I die too," she whispered to him. "I never leave you." She pushed back the damp hair and drew her brown fingers across his forehead with a woman's instinctive caress, smoothing down the refractory hairs of his eyebrows. "The other woman, she no can do that never again.

Si he live, I no do it nothing, but now, si she come,
I kill her by the door."

For this girl, in passion or in suffering, had had
no thought of what is technically known as sin.
A pure child of nature, she had, vital and undy-
ing within her, the instinct of chastity, that tradi-
tional inheritance of woman, transmitted down
through the centuries; and the cold light of intellectual reasoning could never even wither it.
Naturally gifted as she was, she must feel always,
reason never, and there had been no influence in
her plastic years to make unbonded love seem
other than deadly sin. Her conscience had grown
to unblunted maturity and spread its green and
fragrant branches over the clean white flowers of
her soul. Tremaine, in restive hours, had judged
rightly that she could be won only as such women
can be; and, when social ideals were crumbling,
perhaps that alone had cemented his resolution
to go where he could see her no more.

Her eyes fell on the trickling blood again, and
she relaxed her arms and laid him gently on
the ground. She remembered having heard that
a dead man's blood did not flow. She took his

hat and running to the spring behind the house filled it with water. When she returned she put his head on her knee and dashed a palm-full of the water in his face.

He opened his eyes under the shock and looked up vaguely. Then, as sense returned, he remained quiet, gazing into Carmelita's eyes, which revealed more than she knew. For a moment she too was silent, fearful of startling away the returning spirit, then suddenly averted her eyes from the growing power of his, and the blood that had burnt her face receded quickly.

"Your arm hurt?" she asked, her voice cold with the effort to steady it.

"Yes; it is broken."

"The padre—I go for him soon. But first, much better you go in the hut."

"Very well. But you must help me."

He managed to struggle to his feet and drag himself to the hut, then fainted again.

The water revived him after a time, but his head was heavy, and his swollen arm throbbing with pain. He lay for a few moments grasping Carmelita's tightly, then opened his eyes.

"Can you bring me my saddle for a pillow?" he asked.

She went out and unsaddled the mustang, turning the animal loose as she did so. After she had fixed Tremaine's head comfortably he said to her:

"Go now, but don't be long. And get out my revolver before you go.'

She gave him his pistol, put Castro's in her own belt, then left the hut. There was little to be said between them!

Her mustang was tethered at the head of the gulch and she sprang on him and urged the tired animal to a gallop. The padre's house was ten miles away, but she reached it before dark. On her last visit she had been too blind with her own grief to notice the change in him, but she was shocked at his face to-night.

"You are like the old mens," she said. "Padre mio! what is the matter?"

But he would answer none of her questions, and she stated her errand. He heard her listlessly, but promised to go to Tremaine and set his arm.

"I will get Espinoza and a wagon and mattress," he said, "and bring Mr. Tremaine here. He will be more comfortable than at the Aguitas. Now go and take this medicine in case he has fever. It may be morning before I get there, although I shall go as quickly as possible. And take this bread and candle."

The ride back was dark and haunted by many a fear. Just before she reached the gulch the moon, swimming between the great ocean of space and rolling waves of cloud, sent a long beam through the dark currents and made the haunted cañon momentarily alight. A faint wind was swaying the moss that hung from the gaunt branches of the trees on the hills, and the ghostly light gave it a horrid suggestion of human vitality. Carmelita shuddered and crossed herself. She had all the superstition of her race and breeding. Oh! if Tremaine had only gone elsewhere this day. She could have ridden through twenty counties without a qualm. She brought her horse to a halt which nearly unseated her. Something was running down the gulch. Dios! it was the murderer himself. She wheeled her horse about and flew over the road she had come. But only for a moment. With a savage exclamation of dis-

gust she turned again and headed straight for
the hut. Something tottered past her waving its
long arms and crying like a dumb beast in pain.
She sprang from the mustang with half shut-eyes
and panting chest, and rushing into the house,
bolted the door and lit the candle with jumping
fingers. She thrust it hastily upon a shelf and
ran to Tremaine. He was sitting up, watching
her with bright widely opened eyes.

"O señor," she gasped, "si you know how
glad I am you no are sleep! I have so terreeblay
fright. Vasquez—but much better you lie down."

"Do not turn any of them out to-day," he said
unsteadily. "I have something to say to them
first," and he tried to stand up.

"Dios mio"! thought the girl, "he have the de-
lirium, like Jacoba when she have the fever.
Oh, what I do!"

She took him by the arm and forced him back
to his pillow.

"Lie down," she cried peremptorily. "I no let
you move."

He tried to shake her off. "But suppose I
don't want to lie down. Just make this person

let go my other arm, will you? I must be off. I
have something important to say to those men."

"But I want you stay here with me, señor,"
faltered the girl.

"But suppose I don't want to stay with you,
my good girl; what then?"

She bent over him with dilating eyes. "You
no know me? You no know me? Oh, say you
know me and I no care for the rest!"

He looked at her blankly and did not seem disposed to answer at all.

The girl put her lips to his ear.

"Alejandro! Alejandro!" she whispered, "Oh,
you know me, si you no *are* right!"

"I might give them five hundred a piece," he
murmured, "but it seems so paltry. "Oh, if one
could only know what it is best to do." And he
closed his eyes and fell into an uneasy slumber.

Carmelita crept close to him because he was the
only living thing near, not because she felt any
sense of his protection to-night. The wind was
sighing in the cañon. The great willows behind
the hut trailed their branches over the roof with
a slow monotonous scraping. The low boom of

the river came from far, and in the room the sick man muttered. Carmelita made no attempt to sleep. Superstition was quickening every pulse. She dared not move lest again she see Vasquez in the shadows behind her. The candle in the corner looked like a solitary watcher at a wake, and its flame bent and flared as the wind crept through the cracks of the hut—then the shadows danced like the ghosts of the band Vasquez had gathered about him in hell.

The girl put her arid lips to her lover's ear. "Alejandro! Alejandro!" she muttered imploringly. "Come to me. Oh, I am so fright."

"Perhaps, perhaps," muttered Tremaine. "But it seems such a Quixotic thing to do."

A gust of wind came through the window and blew out the candle. It swept cold leaves like dead fingers across the face of the cowering girl and rattled the latch with a long howling wail.

She caught her galloping nerves, and crossing the room lit the candle again.

"Once I think I am brave," she thought hopelessly, "but now I think so great a coward no live. Oh! si he were well. I no care for nothing then—"

She turned quickly with a suppressed cry. Some one was creeping among the stones in front of the hut. An icy sweat burst from every pore of her body. If the steps were Castro's she would be the lioness defending her wounded mate, but against ghosts her spirit offered no bulwark.

The steps shuffled near. They stopped, and a long sighing moan smote on throbbing ears. Carmelita, with hard dilating eyes, stared at the window. Again the stealthy steps approached— no! the thing was *crawling*. Then, a hand, lean, white, nerveless, moved on the low sill and hung limply over. The waves had broken on the shore of the moon's cold domain and the bloodless thing on the sill gleamed in the hard white beams. The hand gave a spasmotic clutch, there was a low gurgling sound, and then, slowly, with painful effort, a white matted head, with gaunt hungry face, raised itself within the aperture and snapped its gums at Carmelita.

The girl broke into wild hysterical weeping.

"Dios mio! Dios mio!" she cried frantically. "It is the old Indian."

She snatched the loaf of bread from the shelf

and flung it through the window, then fell prone
beside Tremaine, her senses at rest.   With an instinctive movement, he put out his arm and drew
her to him, but did not awaken.

XIII.

THE RESPITE.

THE padre and Espinoza arrived at dawn. Carmelita was herself once more, but her eyes were hollow and her face was white. Tremaine was still half-asleep, but no longer muttered.

"Pobrecita! pobrecita!" said Espinoza, patting his niece's forlorn head. "Bad time you have, no? He maka much troubles, mijita?"

She fondled his hand but made no confidence, and in a moment the padre, who was examining Tremaine's arm and chest, called to her to bring him some water.

She watched the priest bind up the wound and gave a little cry as he set the wrist.

"Hurtcha him?" she asked eagerly.

"Yes; but he is the kind to stand it. Give me those bandages."

The padre had studied surgery before coming to this abandoned spot and in a short time Tre-

maine had been skilfully cared for. Then the two
men put him on the mattress and carried him to
the wagon. Carmelita followed and took his head
in her lap, and after a long cold ride Tremaine
was made comfortable in the padre's bed. He sent
word to Hawkins that he had had an accident and
would not be at the Aguitas for a week, but gave
him no particulars.

His fever lasted two days and he slept most of
the time, but on the third he awoke with normal
pulse and a clear head. He felt rather weak, but
the languor in his veins was not unpleasant. As
he opened his eyes Carmelita gave him his medicine and told him that the padre had gone out
and would not return for some hours.

"Thank heaven," he thought, but aloud he said,
"Carmelita, come here."

She took a chair by the bed.

"What I can do?" she asked.

"Give me your hand."

After a moment's hesitation she put her hand
in his. She did not observe that his clasp was
any weaker than when he had sat beside her listening to Enrique's woes.

17

"Tell me, Carmelita, have you forgiven me for being Alexander Tremaine?"

She looked past him at the whitewashed wall by the head of the bed.

"I no know," she said at length. "You no can help, I suppose. And—I no can help too."

"But did you not hate me at first—just after I told you?"

"I no know what I feel then. I—no ask me."

"Tell me another thing; did you follow Castro the other day? It seems hardly possible that you were in the cañon by accident."

"Yes, I follow him all the day, when I find you are out with the sheriffs, and no pay attention to my letter. And jus after you throw the things out of the first hacienda and fright all the mens so they no do it nothing, I am at Miller's house and I hear Castro swear to killing you. So I follow him and I stick him with the knife jus when he throw the rope, so it no go straight. O señor, you know what he do si the rope go right and tie your arms so you no can move? He drag you roun on the groun like you are a calf and whip you and stamp on you and spit in your face. Then

when he have make you so shem you want to die
he shoot you and you no can do it nothing."

Tremaine's face flushed purple at the bare
thought of the indignity he had escaped. And a
woman had saved him from it! But he did not
resent the rescue, for the woman was Carmelita.

"And I give you so much in return!" he answered bitterly after a moment. " I have done so
much good by coming to this ranch!"

" O señor!" cried the girl, the enforced self-
control of the past week beginning to give way,
" *why* we live? why we are make? "

" When a few million more unhappy mortals
have asked that question, Carmelita, perhaps the
Almighty will see fit to answer it," said Tremaine
bitterly. " In the mean time the priests will
stand before their altars and give thanks that the
millions are permitted to suffer."

" But, señor! señor! it is so hard to live fifty,
sixty, years, and in life there no is nothing——"

She sprang to her feet and walked up and down
the little room. " The padre say in life there is
nothing. Geraldina say there no is one thing but
love and that no last. I no know what the other

peoples they do in their lifes to forget what no make them happy to remember, but I see mine. For fifty years I sit sometime in my room and make the closes for the childrens, sometime I kneel in the Mission and pray to die, and sometime I ride to the mountain. Bime by I am too old to ride, and then I only go to the Mission. That, señor, is my life."

"Carmelita, be careful!" Tremaine half sprang from the bed, then sank back again and turned his face to the wall.

She stood beside him. "Forgive me, no?" she said, but her eyes were still flaming and her mouth was tightly set. "I no complain any more. And I have you now. I forget I can think of that while I live. Think, señor, think si you no come! Then I no have nothing to remember." She thought of Geraldine's white face as she spoke, but she would not have given back one of her memories.

He turned suddenly and looked at her with the powerful and penetrating gaze which had convinced so many people of the truth of his words, against their own preconceived ideas.

He spoke deliberately.

"You will forget me," he said. "You are only a child. I am the first man you have seen except your padre and these people you scorn. But that is all. You do not really love me. You will find that out when——"

"What!" cried Carmelita, stung, as all women are, by distrust in the strength of their passion. Her self-control gave way utterly. "You think I no love you? Why, then, you think I lie on the groun all night when you tell me your name and I know you have the wife, and remember I have tell the mens to kill you. Why I beat myself against the earth and beg it to opa and take me down and keep me forever? Why you think I go before it is light to the mountain and beg my redwood to fall on me and kill me si he love me? Why you think I cry and sob till I no have one tear left and my eyes burn like they have the fire in them that eat my heart? Why I hate the birds in the trees I have love before? The padre he tell me to pray, but I no can! The prayer is good when you have live your life, like Geraldina and the padre. It is good when you feel tire out and pray for strength to live; but no when you are young and the heart want another heart like its own. God no can satisfy, then. We no can feel Him, or see Him, or hear Him. He is cold and far and pure like the moon, and that no is what we want when we are young. Si you no have the wife I could love you like the old love God, but si I no can have that I no want nothing else at all." And Carmelita, who had meant to keep her soul in its depths, rushed from the house, and springing on Tremaine's mustang urged him to a wild gallop. When she returned, hours later, physical fatigue had conquered spiritual pain.

XIV.

RICH AND POOR.

A WEEK passed and Tremaine's strength returned in spite of himself. He was in no hurry to get well, but his powerful physique could not be long affected even by a broken arm, and one morning the padre told him that the ride to the Aguitas would not hurt him and that the sheriffs had finished the dispossessing and were awaiting further instructions.

"Very well," said Tremaine shortly. "I will drive over at ten to-night. I do not wish to go before." Then he held out his hand to the priest. "Forgive me," he said, "and let me thank you for your hospitality, poor a return as thanks must be."

"Do not thank me," said the priest. "I did but my duty. But there is one question I wish to ask you, if you will pardon my presumption."

"Ask anything you like." Tremaine pushed a chair to the open window and sat down. Carmelita had gone out and the two men were alone.

"Will you tell me whether you intend doing anything for the wretched people, who at present are herding like so many animals on Mr. Lightfoot's ranch?"

" Yes, I shall do something."

The padre shook his head. " Go and see them before you decide what to do. You do not realize their misery. There are over three hundred of them, men, women, and children, and they are sleeping in the wet grass at night; in the daytime huddling under the trees to escape the scorching sun; the children crying with hunger and running naked with the pigs; the women sunk on the ground in hopeless indifference; the men sullen and cowed out of their manhood. Mr. Tremaine," said the priest, stirred from his apathy by the call of humanity, which alone had power to touch him, " you are a rich man and burdened with a terrible responsibility. You have millions that you took as lightly from your dead father's hand as you accepted the sweetmeats your mother gave you when a child. What can you do with fifteen million dollars? A hundred thousand would supply every want, gratify every ambition—display, and love of power alone excepted. You spend your life in alternate gratification of your petty desires and in revolving plans for the investment of your money. As you sit in your magnificent library, whose luxury must surfeit and weary at times, with your lawyers and agents looking over your deeds and accounts, your leases and mortgages, frowning with annoyance at rents overdue, or thinking uneasily of a great sum in the bank which is bringing no interest, does imagination never picture your mother at the wash-tub, your wife toiling for a dozen clamorous children, sewing, nursing, scrubbing your floors up to the hour of confinement, cooking your wretched dinner with a screaming half-fed child in her arms? When your valet brings the clothes you are to wear at a costly dinner to which rich men flock at your bidding, do you ever amuse yourself picturing a one-roomed hovel of which you are lord, and wherein you sit down to a dinner of greasy meat and boiled potatoes with a lot of half-washed scuffling children, and a hot-faced frowsy wife, cross, sullen, snatching her mouthfuls between the demands of her children? Do you see yourself in a woollen

shirt you have worn for a year, and a pair of overalls stiff with grease and earth, eating your savor-
less meal, too weary in heart and body to make
complaint? When you lie down to rest in a bed
which yields to your body and rests every mus-
cle, do you intensify its luxury by imagining yourself on a filthy pulah mattress, stifling under your
low ceiling, but in your heavy sleep not hearing
even the angry quarrels of your children, crowding into their narrow beds? Forgive me if I have
offended you, but it is time the world should solve
the problem it has wrought. Socialism is a failure; and the further it develops the deeper does
it demonstrate its impotence. It will be a hundred years before Henry George is recognized as
a great man. I see no present solution of a great
and intricate problem but that the rich should
realize their duty to the poor."

Tremaine was not angry, and he had made up
his mind what to do for the squatters; but the
subject was one he was fond of arguing.

"Are you sure we have any duty to the poor?"
he asked. "In this nineteenth century there is no
more excuse for poverty than for certain diseases

in the advanced state of medical science. Intelligence and the commercial instinct have never been
so well and widely developed. It is the exception when the clever man or the industrious man
does not get a competence, whether his sphere be
a large one or a small one. There is no place in
the economy of nature for the man who is not
willing to work, or for the witless. Neither is
there any place for the beggar. When a man
finds that the world has no place for him, either
because he has outgrown usefulness or never had
any, or because he has not been able to make his
friends love him well enough to be eager to keep
him alive, then he should be quietly put out of
the way by the code of the country. The scheme
of creation takes only the race into account, not
the individual. You are a priest, but you are also
an intelligent man, and I don't believe I shock
you. I subscribe to no charitable institutions except those for children; for they—no matter what
their misfortunes of birth—have a future, and only
time can prove whether they are fit to live or not.
I always give a begging woman money because I

am a man, although the same logic applies to either sex; but I never give a nickel to a man."

"Your logic is right," said the priest, who, in spite of himself, felt the stimulus of speaking with a man of his own world once more, "but it would be dangerous to the race to extinguish the instinct of charity—of charity for charity's sake. Human nature would harden without its leavening influence. And, unquestionably, I think you view the matter somewhat brutally. Remember the men who have no chance; men with brains and industry who rot in an old-world city for means to carry them to the new. Not but what the male could work his own way over, but what is he to do with a wife and family of children?"

"He has no business to have either wife or children until he is established in life. There is your 'world's solution of the problem it has wrought;' let procreation halt until the world is large enough once more for its inhabitants. I am not quoting Malthus. Let the marriage ceremony wait. You shake your head at me. Don't talk to me of the sin of ignoring nature. It does not weigh a feather in the scale against the crime of stuffing the world with puny beings whose only resource is to crawl out of life as fast as starvation and disappointment will take them."

" Well, let that point go. Good, or bad, it applies only to the future. What is to be done for the misery of the present? Do you think, yourself, that it is right and just, that a few hundred rich men should hold the world in their hands, should stifle in luxury while the multitude toils; that millions should be at the mercy of the rich for the miserable wages they make?"

" Has it ever occurred to you, that the rich are at the mercy of the poor, not the poor at that of the rich? Who permits us to be rich if not the poor? Who, generation after generation, have slowly and inevitably forged the conditions which allow a man to amass wealth at the expense of his brethren, but the poor—since they represent the great body of humanity? Suppose each man renting a house in San Francisco should suddenly rise and say, 'I will pay no more rent?' Who would compel him? The police? militia? They are included in the renting community. Who would compel them? The army? Suppose the epidemic spread? What chance would the army have against the concerted millions of America? *Then* I should see my mother at the wash-tub, and my wife stewing greasy meat under a cabin roof while I scratched among the potatoes. But that is just where we are safe. There never will be a concerted movement. The timid and the indifferent element are too largely in the majority, and all must take the stand, or none at all. But the fact remains that we rich men hold our wealth because the poor man fosters the conditions which enable us so to do. Why does he foster them? Because he intends to be a rich man himself, some day, and if he destroyed the conditions he would destroy his own hopes. He does not want mediocrity any more than the rich man wants it.

" *He wants to get to the top.*

"Therefore he lets the top alone."

The priest smiled. "That is true," he said almost with enthusiasm, "that is true. I don't pretend to argue the question with you, for I have given it too little study. But I appeal again to your charity, and in spite of your cold-blooded theories, I believe you have a good deal. You intend to do something for these people, and I have a curiosity to know what it is."

" I am perfectly willing to tell you. I shall give them back the land, and divide the rest of the ranch into fifty-acre farms, which I shall give to such applicants as investigation proves are worthy. I say—give them, but I shall retain control for five years, and at the end of that time every lazy man will be turned off. At the same time I will pay the taxes, build the cottages and seed the farms. The scheme interests me. The experiment is a dangerous one; it may be a terrible failure. Suddenly put a hopeless man in possession of a future, and either his self-respect will develop, or a faith in providence which is technically known as laziness. But although I recognize no obligation in the matter, I am glad to give a number of fellow-men that 'chance' in life so often desperately demanded. I shall make the farms as small as possible, however, because the less a man can live comfortably upon, the more contented he is. Place him beyond the limitations of small desires and he wants the earth and is miserable because he can't get it. None of us who are beyond would go down to those conditions, but it is a charity to keep the seeds of discontent in our own small patches, and build a wall about them."

"You will succeed," said the priest, "I feel sure of it, for you have head as well as heart. You will not find much to reward or encourage you at first. These men are sullen and lazy, their characters are grovelling and insensible to all higher instincts. But remember that civilization has barely touched them, that circumstances alone have made them what they are, that under the same conditions you would have been no better. But remember also that if the men are nearly hopeless, a plastic generation is rising ready to be fashioned in the unyielding mould of Circumstance; and I envy you that you have it in your power to decree whether they be animals or self-respecting men. I need not tell you that what energy and life I have left are at your service."

"Yes," said Tremaine, "I rely upon you to be my chief steward, for you can reach these people in many ways that I cannot."

XV.

DIVIDING LINES.

THE stars were thick above the Mission as Tremaine and Carmelita walked up and down the cloisters during the last hour they were to spend together. The light in the girl's eyes was watchful as if the spirit were on unresting guard over the rebellious womanhood which grew with the demand for its surrender. During the last few days she had not spoken of herself, and Tremaine, with returning strength, had been equally shy of the subject. He had asked her many questions about the squatters, and slight as was her personal acquaintance with them, there was little she could not tell of their habits and characters.

They had not spoken for some time, but suddenly he gave an impatient sigh, and turned to her.

"I never felt less like talking business," he said, "but I have something to say to you and it must be said now, for I shall not see you again."

18

She looked hard at the grim walls of the Mission opposite, but made no reply.

"I cannot give you happiness, my dear; I have brought you only misery. But this I will do in commemoration of you: the squatters shall have their homes and I shall divide the rest of the ranch among those who will make the best use of it. I say I do this in commemoration of you," he said turning to the astounded and enraptured girl, "but I am bound to confess that I am glad of the occupation and interest it will give me. Are you satisfied with me, Carmelita? You were very hard upon me once, I remember. You told me some pretty sharp home truths during that first interview of ours. But if there is anything more you want you shall have it."

She looked back at him with eyes in which the watch-fires had suddenly died.

"Señor," she said, "you make me glad, you have make me suffer. I no can say no more."

Tremaine turned from her quickly. He had that self-control which only passionate men do have, until they see fit to let it go, when its very memory cowers afar, forlorn, with trailing wings.

The attempt to be business-like made him brusque. "This scheme will have its consolation for you——" he was beginning, when she interrupted him eagerly.

"Señor, there *is* one more thing."

"What is it? I shall have more happiness in giving than you in taking."

"Buy the forest on the mountain. Si you take care the mens take care the trees too. It kill me si they are cut down."

"I will buy the redwoods and you shall never see an axe in the forest again. But to go back to what I was saying. I wish you to be the leading spirit here. Your Geraldine, whoever she may be, has taught you the meaning of the word society. Form one here so that these people will take an interest in each other. Society developed that far is a virtue; a step further and it is a vice. You do not understand, Carmelita, and, thank heaven, you never will. But make them meet and be gay together. Have pic-nics (they are primitive enough to enjoy them) and dances. Make each wedding an event; I will give every girl her wedding-gown. Spur their ambition and make them

go to school. I put you and the padre in charge
of the ranch for I shall not return. He will send
me a report four times a year and you will send
me a demand for everything you want done. One
day there will be a town here and you will be respected and remembered as its patron saint."

The girl's face flushed and sparkled. Her heart
folded its wings for a moment.

"O señor! señor!" she cried. "I can do all
that! There go to be something in the life!"

She looked past him dreamily. A measure of
compensation had come to her and there was some
light in the future. It was as if a pink glow had
suffused the gray plain the priest had pictured,
and sparks were bursting through the ashes beneath the smiles of the passing souls above.

Tremaine held out his hand.

"Good-by," he said.

She looked at him blankly—then remembered.
The pink glow vanished, the world was gray. She
touched his hand with her cold fingers.

"Good-by," she said. Then appalled, broken,
she flung herself upon him pressing her ams convulsively about him. "O my redwood! my red-

wood!" she sobbed wildly, "give to me the strength, the comfort! I no can bear alone! Help me to stand. Oh, put your arms around me, and then I no care, they are so strong."

Tremaine bent his head and the Mission threw its shadow over his white face and dilating nostrils. His arm curved rigidly about her, but he pressed her tenderly and said comforting words.

She threw herself back against his arm and lifted her wet face. "I no could help," she sobbed, "I no could help. I no can stand alone like before, and no one is strong like you. *You* are the tree now. He no will be the same again. Oh! Alejandro, *why* we are make?"

"You will never be alone. Think and believe that I am with you always. You will never be out of my mind for an hour at a time. You have my heart and my soul. Now go, Carmelita."

A wagon rattled out of the padre's corral. Tremaine stood listening to the wild thumping of a mustang's hoofs, dying in the distance.

XVI.

PEACE.

GERALDINE lay on the divan watching the sun
slip over the mountain. Once she held her hand
up to the parting rays and fancied they wandered
through. Her face was white as the azaleas beneath her window and her mouth was like their
withered petals. Her youth had gone, but it left
no pang. Nor did she suffer. In the days and
nights which had passed since she spoke with the
priest, vitality had burned to its embers and rest
had come. Each mortal has one central interest
which binds him to life. The priest had put the
period to this woman's, and did she live through
eternity, the dim lamp in her soul would never
give a flicker nor send a ripple through her veins.
Her heart was not even sad; it pulsed haltingly
though its numbered beats.

The door opened, and the woman turned her
head. An old man, with cold calm spiritual face

entered and stood beside her. She held out her
hand, but no color touched her face. Had he
come with the youth and ardor of their first hour's
passion he could not have stirred her.

The priest took her hand and looked into her
calm eyes. "I have come," he said, "to tell you
that the struggle is over, that the man is dead,
and the priest alone remains. I have thought it
best to tell you this that you might have one reproach less on your soul. During these days I
have plucked memory up by her roots; I have
pinched imagination to death between my fingers
as I would snuff out a candle; I have dug a grave
and buried passion. Now, for the first time, I am
equipped for my work, for the first time I can
hope for forgiveness for the sins of my youth. I
can pray for your soul as well as mine, and I believe that our sin will be forgiven us."

The woman moved her head, her eyes wandering to the golden mountains. Where was her
lover? Waiting far back on the shores of youth?
A man is more than one being in his life. If the
last persists, why not the first? If there be a hereafter for his age, why not for his youth?

"Is religion impossible without fanaticism?" she said faintly. "It was not sin. You had not been ordained, your future was still your own, and man was not made to live on dogmas. And your church—our church, if you will, for it holds me, too—should be satisfied. If I betrayed one of its poor secrets that slipped your tongue, I betrayed it through ignorance of its awful significance, and I have been punished! I could not foresee the terrible consequences. The most terrible to me has been that you loved your religion better than me. I could have stood the separation, since it was inevitable, but not that."

"I have not come to reproach you further. The fault was mine from the beginning. I broke the vows my spirit, if not my tongue, had made."

She smiled at the swimming mountains, vague and exquisite as the memories of the past.

"Yes," she murmured, "thank God you did."

The priest sighed and bent over her. "I go, Geraldine. But let me speak to you first as priest to penitent. The world has no longer a place for you. Give your soul and energies to the church. Spend your life at the foot of the cross, praying for the sins of mankind. For every prayer offered up on naked knees, aching through a winter's night on a stone floor, shall a woman's erring soul be reclaimed. I know a beautiful convent, Geraldine, in the heart of Europe, whose gardens are like the groves of paradise, leading the thoughts to celestial gates. The lilies lie on the lake and the gray stone walls thrust their rough old stones through swarming green. The chapel is arched and dim, and the nuns kneel in their oaken stalls and chant like a celestial choir, while the incense floats above and wreathes the pictured windows. Do you remember the chorus of nuns in Chopin's nocturne? In those moments your spirit will faint with heavenly ecstasy; you will know a delicious foretaste of the joy to come. But the cells are cold and bare, and on their stones you will mortify the flesh, and your spirit will wail for the redemption of the world. This is the life for you, Geraldine. Give me your promise to go and I will write to-morrow to the reverend mother."

But Geraldine, still with that smile of perfect peace on her cold lips, had gone down into the shadowy valley, to dwell forever by that quiet river whose voice would chant dear memories. .

XVII.

As Tremaine stood on the porch of the Aguitas waiting for the stage which would carry him back to civilization, his eyes were suddenly arrested by an object far down the road he was to traverse. It looked like a small pink cloud which had floated on from sunrise. Directly beneath the cloud—which, by the way, was floating toward the Aguitas—was another object that looked much like a wagon drawn by a pair of spanking horses. Tremaine levelled his field glass at the approaching phenomenon. Yes, it certainly was a wagon, and those horses were not mustangs. And—yes—the pink cloud was a parasol.

He lowered his glass with a laugh. "Rather a refreshing sight," he thought, "but so incongruous that it is almost a parody."

He walked up and down the porch, idly watching the approaching wagon when his steps turned

him toward it. Some people were doubtless travelling in their own conveyance to the hot springs
in the south. As the wagon came nearer he could
make out that a woman in it wore a dress of silver gray, and later, that she had fair hair. Suddenly he stopped short, his heavy eyes opening
wide with an angry gleam.

"Jimminy Creepers," exclaimed Hawkins, who
was sitting on a barrel chewing tobacco, "if it ain't
Missis Tremaine."

Mrs. Termaine it was. She drove up, smiling,
fresh and dainty as the wild flowers she had not
deigned to notice. As she saw Tremaine she wafted
him a kiss with her little gray fingers, and seemed
not at all disconcerted by his lack of enthusiasm.

"You wouldn't answer my letters to say I could
come," she cried, with her infantile pout, "so I
made up my mind to do as I pleased for once. I
was determined to see this place, and have a look
at the picturesque Californian. Do they wear
sombreros and ponchos? What is the matter with
your arm?" And she sprang lightly past Tremaine's hand, followed by her less agile maid.

"I hurt it. You have selected an unfortunate

time," added her husband coldly. "I return by
the stage to day."

"No! no! you must not go," she said coaxingly, "I am too tired to go back to-day. Just
think!—I have driven thirty miles. Why can't
they run the trains this way? You would not be
so *cruel* as to take me right back."

Tremaine hesitated. It would be rather brutal.
"Very well," he said finally, "I will stay over until to-morrow; but you must go then. I have im-
perative business; and I do not suppose you wish
to stay here alone."

"Of course not, although if I had known you
would be so selfish I should have brought a lot
of people and we could have entertained each
other. I would have brought them, anyhow, but
I was not sure of the accommodations. I suppose
you have something for me to eat and a place
where I can rest."

"I beg your pardon," and he opened the door
of his room. "You can have this. There is another
vacant, I believe, but this is the more comfortable.
You will have to leave the door open or keep
your lamp lit, however, for there is no window."

"No what? but that is too funny. I shall have an experience to relate when I go home. A room without a window!"

Her maid fixed her comfortably on the bed, and Tremaine sent her some fried steak and cold apple pie, upon which the landlady had placed a large slice of butter. She discarded the butter with a wry face, but being hungry, managed to eat the rest, and then slept like an infant for a couple of hours. At the end of that time she felt like a morning rose and returned to the porch where her unwilling lord was awaiting her.

"I want to be amused, Alex," she said plaintively. "Take me somewhere. I want to see the place and the people. If you make me go back to-morrow it is your duty to entertain me to-day. Do they all live in one room?"

Tremaine groaned in spirit. He did not feel in an amusing vein, and his wife was the last person on earth he wanted to talk to. And to drive with her about this ranch!

"You would not find these people interesting, and the roads are very rough," he was beginning, when Hawkins came to the rescue.

"If you will excuse my officiousness, sir," he said, tipping his hat, "I would suggest as how you took Missis Tremaine to see the cattle brandin' over to Lightfoot's. It's only a matter of six miles and she kin stay there all night. If you don't want to go, I would like nothin' better'n to take her, as I'd like to see the round-up myself."

Tremaine caught eagerly at the proposition.

"Yes, go, Adelaide," he said. "There is an experience, if you want one, and will give you something to talk about. The Mexican is picturesque on horseback, if anywhere, and Lightfoot has the finest cattle in the valley."

Mrs. Tremaine needed no urging; the proposition had fascinated her at once. She rose to her feet and tied the strings of her bonnet.

"Do we go now?" she asked.

"Yes, ma'am, we hav'n't no time to lose and it's one o'clock now. I'll put two fresh mustangs in that ere light wagon you brought and we'll be off in fifteen minutes."

"Have you been ill," demanded Mrs. Tremaine of her husband, as they walked back and forth, awaiting Hawkins' return. "You are rather pale

and you look quite different—1 can hardly say
how; but you do."

"I had some fever, but I am well enough now."

"Did you have much trouble with these people?
Have they all gone?"

"They went, but they come back to-morrow; I
will explain when we return to town. I do not
feel in a humor for talking business to-day."

Mrs. Tremaine lifted her pretty little pink chin,
"Well, one thing is certain; dispossessing squatters has not improved your temper. You are as
cross as a bear."

"I am not cross, but it has annoyed me to be
obliged to defer my return to town. Are you sure
you are too tired for the trip? It is not too late."

He remembered afterward that her curved little
mouth had never set itself in a more determined
line as she looked past him at the approaching
wagon and replied with her babyish inflection.

"Yes."

He shrugged his shoulders impatiently and
helped her into the wagon, then felt some com-
punction for his abruptness.

"Take good care of yourself," he said, as he

wrapped the linen dust cloth about her. "The roads have been badly cut up by the heavy rains and you will be a good deal jolted. Hold on when you come to the bad places. Shall I raise your parasol for you?"

"No, thanks. Good-by," and Mrs. Tremaine, whose temper was rarely ruffled, gave him a charming smile and drove off under her pink canopy, regarded with awe and admiration by the habitués of the Aguitas.

"Would you like to see Poverty Flat, Missis?" asked Hawkins.

"Poverty Flat?"

"That's what they call the place where the squatters is camped. I suppose Mister Tremaine's told you that he's give them all their farms."

"He's done what?"

"Give 'em to 'em, out and out, or will at the end of five years, and is agoin' to pay the taxes to boot. The sheriff has cleared out in disgust. I don't mean to pass any remarks myself, and Mister Tremaine's old enough to know his own bizness best, but I'll be doggoned if I kin help doin' a heap o' thinkin'."

"I am sure you must be mistaken. Mr. Tremaine is considered an unusually good business man. How many of them are there? I suppose they could all be put at one end of the ranch so that they wouldn't interfere with us."

Hawkins knew that he had no right to gossip about Tremaine's plans, even to his wife, but the temptation to communicate the astounding news was too great to be resisted.

"Well you see, Missis," he said, "you ain't heard the wust yet—not by a long shot. Mister Tremaine is goin' to send down two surveyors to stake off the ranch into fifty-acre farms, and I've got orders to give any man possession who comes down with a certificate from him. There ain't no use mincin' the truth, he's goin' to give this eligant ranch, fifty thousand acres, clean away, and I for one call it a damned shame. Excuse me, Missis, but I do. Remember I've knowed Mister Tremaine man and boy."

Adelaide turned white about her lips. "And I am not going to have my Spanish house and English park," she said, unconsciously stating her grievance aloud. "He is going to give this magnificent place, *that he paid two hundred and twenty thousand dollars for*, to a lot of common ignorant Irish emigrants and dirty natives. He shall not! I will not let him."

Hawkins shook his head. " I don't kalkilate you can do any good, Missis. Mister Tremaine's pretty set in his ways, once he takes a streak. The deed's done."

" He will be the laughing stock of San Francisco," exclaimed Adelaide, another phase of the calamity presenting itself. " The papers will fairly hoot at him. I won't stay in the town. But I always knew he'd do something ridiculous. Under all that sleepy indifference, there are a lot of old-fashioned notions and absurd impulses. I only wonder he hasn't presented his whole fortune to the State and turned me out into the street." In the bitterness of her grief she felt almost confidential toward the disapproving servitor.

" I sympathize with you, ma'am. I do indeed. But there's Poverty Flat, if you'd like to see it. I felt rather sorry for 'em before, but I'll be hanged if I do now."

Mrs. Tremaine turned her head and looked

through shining angry eyes at the wretched en-
campment by the roadside.

"I do not wish to stop," she said. "They are
not even picturesque. Look at those dirty little
naked children playing with the pigs! It's indecent. And those fat women are really horrible.
Tremaine had better buy them some corsets." She
had the latent vulgarity of all cold natures, but
she would have attributed its manifestation to the
revolt of outraged refinement.

Hawkins thought her very witty and laughed
heartily. "That ud be throwin' jewels to swine,
sure enough. They never seen corsets in their
born days. This is the Rancho de los Colmenares
—means Ranch of the bee-hives, and belongs to
Mr. Lightfoot. He's got about sixty thousand
acres, but the ranch ain't a circumstance to the
Cerritos for beauty. It's mostly flat, you see, but
its a bully farm for raisin' cattle. Mr. Lightfoot
must have made a good pile last year. It's a big
payin' business, I tell you what."

Mrs. Tremaine was beginning to tire of the
agent's attempts to entertain her, and retiring
within herself, meditated upon her wrongs. She

had one compensation in store. Several times during her married life she had given Tremaine an extremely uncomfortable fifteen minutes. She decided that when she returned to the Cerritos to-morrow morning he should feel as if he were being slowly crushed in an ice-field. That was one of her accomplishments, and she was proud of it.

The wagon jolted heavily over the rough road and she wished that she had not come. Her back ached and the sun blazed through her thin parasol.

"How many more miles have we?" she asked.

"We'll be there in ten minutes, Missis," and Adelaide, tipping back her sunshade, saw, about a quarter of a mile away, a large adobe house with a rude garden about it, and, at the back, a large corral and a field of cattle.

"They're roundin'-up now," continued Hawkins. "We're in good time for the brandin'."

The road took them by the field and Adelaide looked with some interest at the army of red and white animals with their tossing horns. A number of vaqueros were galloping about shouting at the cattle and trying to press them into rank.

"By Golly!" exclaimed Hawkins suddenly,

"if there ain't Castro. Well, of all the gall, and a sheriff after him. And there's Espinoza too."

As Castro saw Hawkins he spurred his horse and rode up to him. The scowl on his face was heavier than usual.

"Whatte this I hear?" he demanded. "Espinoza go to keep his hacienda?"

Hawkins gave a grunt. He was not afraid of Castro, with a half dozen other men in sight. "What's that your bizness?"

"Tella me si it is true?" roared Casto. "Diablo! whatte he do for the Señor Tremaine to getta his ranchita when the others live in the mud? He give to him Car——"

"Shut up!" interrupted Hawkins, and he drove off. Castro sent a volley of curses after him, then wheeled and galloped directly over to Espinoza.

Hawkins drove the wagon into the shed and lifted Mrs. Tremaine to the ground.

"You won't mind walkin' a bit? But there's no safe place to tie the horses near the corral."

"I am glad to walk," she said, and moving lightly over the ground, she looked like an animated silver statue topped by a big pink rose.

The sun beat full upon her, and as she walked up
the road toward the corral Lightfoot and his vaqueros stopped a moment to look at her.

"Who's the visitor?" asked the master curious-
ly. "Looks like 'Frisco. That's Tremaine's agent
with 'er. Blowed if I kin be bothered with 'er,
though, and Mrs. L.'s away. Here, Castro, stop
your rowing with Espinoza and help round up
these cattle. They're as obstinate as mules to-day.
Rope that girl over there. She's been behavin'
like hell all mornin', and they'll be makin' a break
fust thing you know. Here! none o' that ——"

But before the words were out of his mouth,
Castro had snatched his pistol from his belt and
discharged it at Espinoza. The shot missed its
mark, but struck a steer just behind. With a furious bellow the animal reared and struck a neighbor with its forefeet. In a second terror and
fury had run like an electric wave over the whole
body of cattle.

"My God!" cried Lightfoot, "there's goin' to
be trouble."

The cattle were seething and trampling, stumbling against each other and rushing aimlessly from

right to left. Castro, seeing what he had done, felt a brute desire to show these angry beasts with their ominous mutterings that he was master. With a hoarse cry which every one of them understood he dashed along their front, vociferating at them like a furious general at a cowardly army. For a second the cattle shrank, then blind terror possessed them once more. He was too late. The smell of blood was in their nostrils!

Suddenly their aimless trampling ceased. One in the front rank had caught sight of the brilliant pink and silver object coming up the road. Then purpose entered into his madness, and with a furious bellow he made straight for the open. Lightfoot and his men yelled with horror. The former raised himself in his stirrups and waved his hat frantically at the stupefied woman, pointing toward his house. Castro was half way across the field when the concerted movement took place. As he saw that a stampede was inevitable he turned with an oath and dashed down the road. Hawkins had caught Mrs. Tremaine by the hand and was running across the open in the poor hope of getting beyond the cattles' flank before they should have time to turn. Adelaide gave one terrified glance over her shoulder, then shut her eyes and stumbled after Hawkins. But still she saw those tossing horns like gaunt skeleton fingers, those flaming eyes and frothing mouths. Castro, yelling frantically, neared them. His horse shied violently at a large pink object on the ground, reared at the vicious pull on his cruel bit, stumbled and went down with the cursing Mexican in a cloud of dust. The harsh, horrified shouts of Lightfoot and his men, the hoarse protest of one doomed man, the gurgling curses of another as he tore the ground with teeth and nails, the shrill hopeless scream of a woman, and the cattle, close in their ranks as an army which was to decide the fate of a nation, swept over the shaking miles.

And where a moment before had been two strong men and one fair woman, was a pulpy mass of flesh and cloth trampled down into the ever waiting, all receiving earth.

THE LITANY OF THE REDWOODS.

THE LITANY OF THE REDWOODS.

A LIGHT fall of snow had drifted through the redwood tops and powdered the brown pine needles. The squirrels chatted in their hidden store rooms, and the deer leaped in the keen bright air. The redwoods, gray and stern, set their heads against the coming blasts and braced their rigid arms. They might succumb to man and steel, but Nature had no enemy to pit against them.

Carmelita lay at the foot of her redwood. She did not feel so intimate with him as of old, but she loved him for remembrance' sake and he was her only friend. For she was very lonely. Geraldine had gone. The padre was like a passing ghost. She had not heard from Tremaine since she had bidden him good-by in the Mission's cloister. She had sternly put aside all insistent hopes born of his wife's horrible death, but that he loved her and that she would see him again she never doubted. Not a mile from her tree, in the very heart of the forest, an immense adobe house had been built on a cliff above the creek. Men had come from the city and furnished it, and an old couple had been placed in charge. Carmelita knew that sooner or later Tremaine would come and live in that house; but at this point her future's perspective closed suddenly. Every evening she spent an hour in the cloisters of the Mission and Tremaine was with her then.

She raised her head. A horseman was coming up the road; the dry branches were crackling under the mustang's feet. She sat up with a frown. This was her own domain and no one had ever passed this way before. It must be one of the new farmers, and for a moment her philanthropy was threatened.

The horse toiled up the steep road, and through the trees she saw him round the gulch. She sprang to her feet, the breath struggling in her throat. Horse and rider passed behind a clump of trees, then reappeared a few feet away, and Carmelita turned and pressed her face to her tree.

Tremaine threw the bridle over the horse's neck

and came to her. He took her to him and kissed
her face and mouth until the girl lay heavy in his
arms, her fingers drawn to her palms with pain in
their tips. He unbraided her hair and cast it
about her. "That is the way I always see you,"
he said, his own voice shaking, "only it should
drift over a long, white gown. We will be married in the old Mission by your padre, and the
house by the creek is ready for us."

He pushed his hand through her warm hair,
but looked past her awakening eyes. "I have a
plan of life to propose to you," he went on steady-
ing his voice. "I have given it much thought in
lonely nights since we parted; but I have lived
widely, I have known the redwoods, and I think
I am right. I want you to have no friend, not
even an acquaintance, but myself; that is, of our
station in life. We have both work to do among
these squatters. But you must have no one to
depend upon for your pleasure, your diversion,
your entertainment, or happiness, you must have
no companion but myself. This is not jealousy,
Carmelita, unless it be a jealous desire for your
good. I have drunk of all the wines that flow

from the fountain of life. There is nothing in society, nothing in friendship, nothing even in personal contact with great minds. Their written words are always the best part of them. Friends have other friends, or when they do not betray or scratch they weary with the minds we have exhausted. Society is a bubble to be pricked, not blown. So I have come to this conclusion: that the only chance of happiness lies in the isolated companionship of mated souls. Nor can I see anything selfish in such a life. I fail to remember ever having done any man good by listening to his tiresome opinions or to his string of woes that he had poured into a dozen ears before mine. But let that go. Later—in a year or two—you shall see all that the best part of the world has to offer. Does all this sound selfish to you, Carmelita? Aside from my own desires, I have planned for your good with all the sense and experience I possess. With people in general you have nothing in common, and in that minor world we call society you would be wretched and disgusted. You would not understand nor be understood. But 'life' in its free and educating sense you shall know and feel that no woman stands before you. My God! what a woman you will make."

He went on dreamily, his face against hers. "Is there one woman who will look at life through the eyes of her lover and not insist upon nibbling every apple until each fine flower of her nature is brown and curled at the edges? Shall we live in this forest until we have absorbed its mighty symbolism and the mystery of the redwoods? We shall know that primeval union——"

He unclasped his arms and pushed her back against the tree, looking full into her eyes.

"Tell me that you love me," he said. "Quick!"

She gazed at him for a moment with languid eyes and parted lips. Then a great flame burst from her heart and swept through her body. She gave a loud, ecstatic cry, like a lioness who has found her mate.

"Alejandro! Alejandro! *I love you!*"

And she flung her arms about him and kissed him full on the mouth.

He staggered under her passionate lips as he had not when Castro's arms had crushed him, and his self-control gave way. He caught her in a

sudden, hard embrace and kissed her until the
mountain reeled beneath them and the forest hum
dinned in their ears as if all the sounds of earth
were in that lonely spot.

"I say before to myself, but no like this," she
panted, shaking in his arms, then said no more.

But the redwood sighed, for his heart was lonely.

THE END.